Magical Tales

for young readers

THIS IS A PARRAGON BOOK

© Parragon 1998

Parragon
13 Whiteladies Road, Clifton, Bristol BS8 1PB

Produced by
The Templar Company plc,
Pippbrook Mill, London Road, Dorking,
Surrey RH4 1JE

Printed in Italy

ISBN 0 75252 837 8

Illustrated by:
Diana Catchpole, Robin Edmonds, Paul Gamble, Phil Garner, Claire Mumford,
Jenny Press, Lesley Smith, Jane Taylor

Magical Tales

for young readers

PARRAGON

This book belongs to

Gemma   Ferguson

Contents

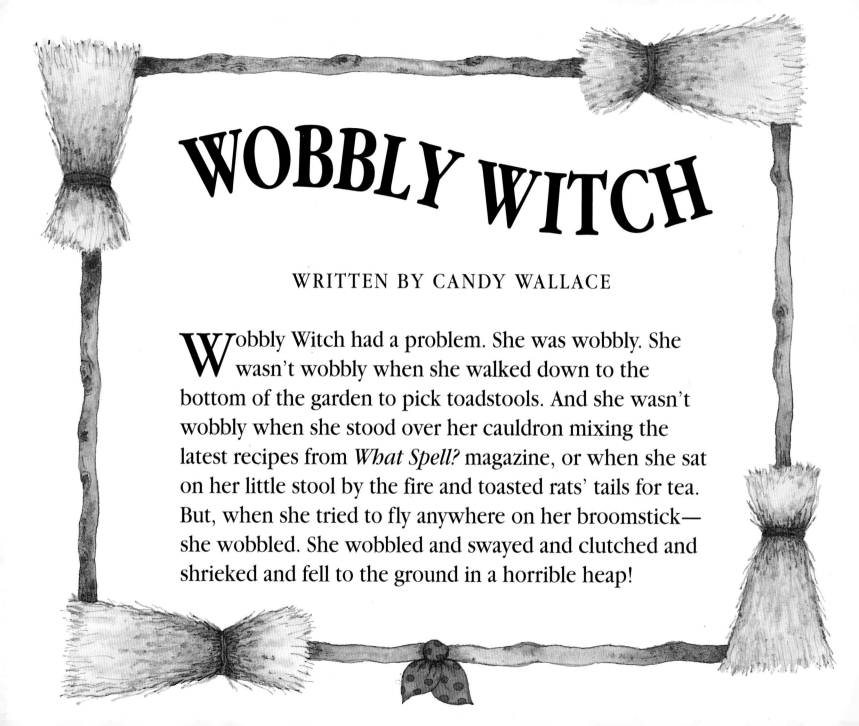

WOBBLY WITCH

WRITTEN BY CANDY WALLACE

Wobbly Witch had a problem. She was wobbly. She wasn't wobbly when she walked down to the bottom of the garden to pick toadstools. And she wasn't wobbly when she stood over her cauldron mixing the latest recipes from *What Spell?* magazine, or when she sat on her little stool by the fire and toasted rats' tails for tea. But, when she tried to fly anywhere on her broomstick— she wobbled. She wobbled and swayed and clutched and shrieked and fell to the ground in a horrible heap!

Poor Wobbly had never learned to fly a broomstick. Some witches took to it like a duck to water and never needed a single lesson. Others went to the *Sky's The Limit School of Broomstick Flying*. But Wobbly just couldn't be bothered to learn when she was young and now she was too proud to admit that she couldn't fly. She told all her friends that she'd lost her broomstick.

So Wobbly had to go everywhere on the bus. It was very embarrassing and most inconvenient. How would you feel if you had to sit on a bus in your pointy black hat with horrid schoolboys making rude remarks about your funny nose? She even had to go to the W.I. (the Witches' Institute) on the bus. All the others flew in on smart broomsticks. Wobbly felt quite left out as they discussed the special features of their latest models.

"Mine does 0–60 in ten seconds," said Edna.

Wobbly might never have learned to fly, if it hadn't been for the birthday present and her cat, Boris.

On Wobbly's birthday the postman brought lots of lovely birthday cards, a couple of small parcels and one big one that was very long and very thin. One parcel had a smart new witch's hat in it, from Wobbly's friend Vera.

The other one was a silver balloon on a string. It had "Happy Birthday!" on it and floated up into the air when she opened the parcel. Wobbly was very pleased.

"Now what can this long one be, Boris?" said Wobbly to her cat, who, like all cats was very curious. Boris snuggled up to Wobbly and purred. He'd had a large kipper for breakfast and was in a very good mood.

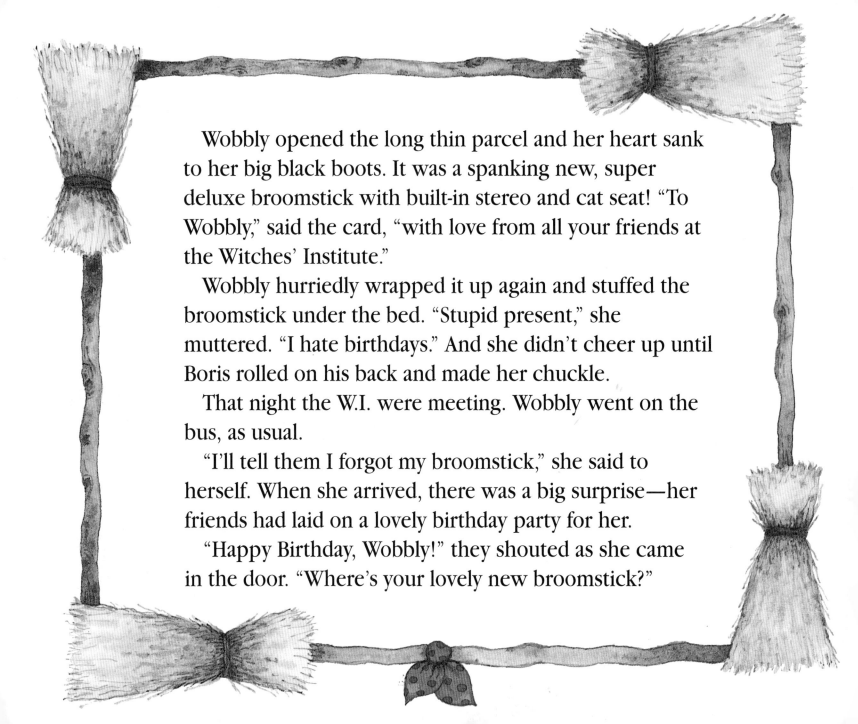

Wobbly opened the long thin parcel and her heart sank to her big black boots. It was a spanking new, super deluxe broomstick with built-in stereo and cat seat! "To Wobbly," said the card, "with love from all your friends at the Witches' Institute."

Wobbly hurriedly wrapped it up again and stuffed the broomstick under the bed. "Stupid present," she muttered. "I hate birthdays." And she didn't cheer up until Boris rolled on his back and made her chuckle.

That night the W.I. were meeting. Wobbly went on the bus, as usual.

"I'll tell them I forgot my broomstick," she said to herself. When she arrived, there was a big surprise—her friends had laid on a lovely birthday party for her.

"Happy Birthday, Wobbly!" they shouted as she came in the door. "Where's your lovely new broomstick?"

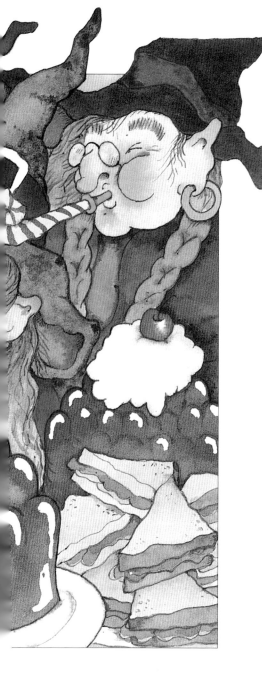

Wobbly soon forgot to feel miserable. There was a huge birthday cake decorated with little bats made out of icing. There were extra wobbly jellies in her honour and lots of delicious sandwiches. It all went well, until somebody mentioned playing games.

They played Hide and Shriek, Pass the Toad and Pin the Tail on the Rat. But the next game was Broomstick Races. Soon, all the witches but Wobbly were whizzing up and down on their broomsticks, cackling and having fun. Wobbly looked on and sulked.

"Right, that's it!" she said. "I'm going home. I hate parties!" And she sneaked out.

When she arrived home, she expected Boris to meet her at the door. But there was no sign of him.

"Great lazy lump," thought Wobbly, crossly. "He's still sleeping off that kipper I gave him!" But when she looked on his favourite chair, he wasn't there. "Boris, Boris, where are you?" she called. But there was no answering miaow.

Feeling worried, Wobbly went outside and called his name again. It was a dark night with a bright, shiny moon and she strained her eyes to see. Then something caught her eye. Right at the top of a tree, she saw a flash of light. It was her birthday balloon, caught on a branch. Suddenly, the branch shook.

"Miaeeeeew!" It was Boris! He had chased the balloon to the top of the tallest tree in the garden and now he was stuck!

"Oh, you silly cat!" shrieked Wobbly. "How am I going to get you down from there!"

"Miaeeeeew!" wailed poor Boris.

Wobbly rushed to fetch an old ladder. But when she put it against the tree it didn't even reach half way up. Poor Boris seemed to be clinging on by a claw. His miaows grew fainter…

Wobbly stamped her foot and turned and rushed into her cottage. She dashed up the stairs and into the bedroom.

On her hands and knees, she grabbed the parcel under the bed and hurried downstairs with it, tearing off the paper as she went.

"Don't worry, Boris!" she cried. "I'll rescue you!" Leaping astride the gleaming new broomstick, she closed her eyes and took a deep breath…

Up she went, up into the sky without a single wobble! As she climbed higher and higher, her old hat blew off and was carried away by the wind. The broomstick swept round in a curve and came to a stop, hovering over the branch where poor Boris was clinging on for dear life.

Wobbly grabbed him and put him on the broomstick behind her. Then she untangled the balloon, tied it to the broomstick and swept down to a smooth landing outside her front door. Boris walked off the broomstick as if nothing had happened.

Wobbly leapt off and skipped and hopped with glee.

"Did you see that, Boris!" she cackled. "I can fly, I can fly! Come on!" She ran into the cottage and grabbed her new hat. "We have a party to go to!"

They jumped back on and took off.

"I've fetched my new broomstick!" cried Wobbly as she arrived at the party. They were still racing broomsticks and hadn't even noticed she was gone! Wobbly and Boris joined in and won two races! As they flew home after the party, Wobbly looked down at the bus below and chuckled.

"I couldn't fly because I was afraid," she said to Boris, who sat purring behind her. "But tonight I was so worried you would fall and hurt yourself—I forgot to be afraid!"

From that day on, Wobbly flew everywhere on her smart new broomstick. She's still called Wobbly, but she doesn't wobble any more!

A WISH TOO FAR

WRITTEN BY DAVE KING

Nathan was bored. He wasn't just bored in that "Ho Hum! I haven't got a thing to do!" kind of way that most of us feel every now and then. Oh no, he was bored in a full blown, major league, top of the list, wet Sunday afternoon in a boring seaside town kind of way, that makes you pace around for an hour and a half before screaming, "IIIIII'm boooorrred!!" at the top of your voice.

Strangely enough, it was a wet Sunday afternoon in a boring seaside town. Nathan's parents had brought him

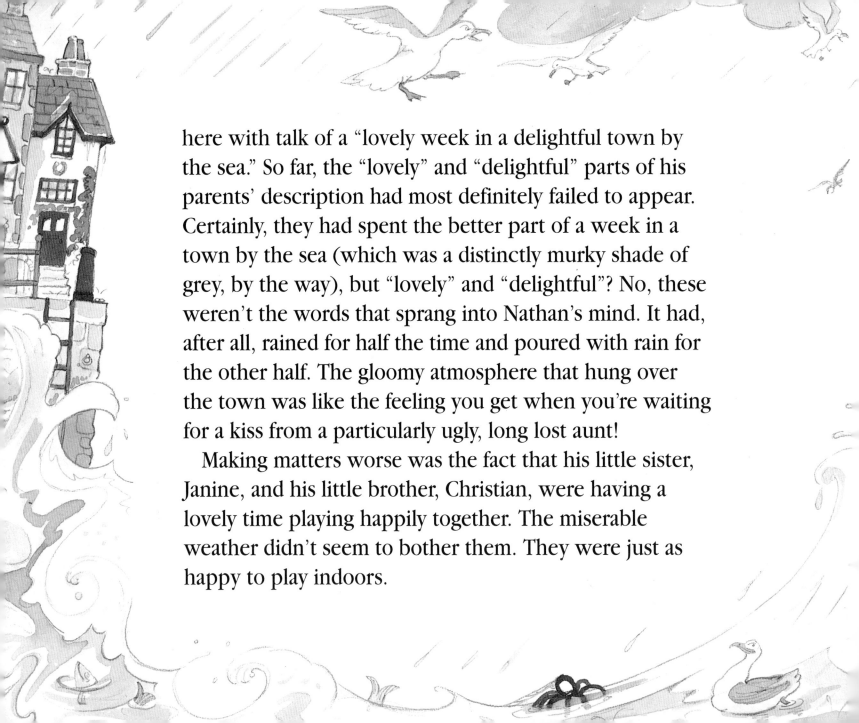

here with talk of a "lovely week in a delightful town by the sea." So far, the "lovely" and "delightful" parts of his parents' description had most definitely failed to appear. Certainly, they had spent the better part of a week in a town by the sea (which was a distinctly murky shade of grey, by the way), but "lovely" and "delightful"? No, these weren't the words that sprang into Nathan's mind. It had, after all, rained for half the time and poured with rain for the other half. The gloomy atmosphere that hung over the town was like the feeling you get when you're waiting for a kiss from a particularly ugly, long lost aunt!

Making matters worse was the fact that his little sister, Janine, and his little brother, Christian, were having a lovely time playing happily together. The miserable weather didn't seem to bother them. They were just as happy to play indoors.

Nathan just wanted the holiday to be over and to get back home. Unfortunately, they still had another two days to go. Nathan paced up and down, sat grumpily in a chair (ignoring the book that his dad had bought for him), or sat in front of the television, flicking between the channels. And still the rain pitter-pattered against the window.

"I wish I could be on my own somewhere, without my family getting under my feet!" he thought, gloomily.

Finally, he got up and grabbed his coat. "Where are you going?" asked his mum.

"Into the garden!" he replied.

His mum sighed wearily. "But it's still raining!"

Nathan put on his coat.

"I don't care!" he said. "I'm going to stand in the garden and grow roots and become a tree and then I'll be stuck here for ever!" And with that, he stomped out.

"Cor!" said Janine, excitedly. "That sounds brilliant! Come on, Chris, let's go and watch!"

Out in the garden, Nathan splashed across the muddy grass with his sister and brother following closely behind. As they neared the far end of the garden, Nathan turned to the others and began to snarl at them, continuing to walk backwards as he did so.

"Why don't you leave me alone?" he snapped.

"We want to see you turn into a tree!" Christian replied.

"Ohhh… that's all I need…" Nathan began, but was cut off as he disappeared from sight. Janine and Christian stopped in their tracks.

They looked down and saw a hole in the ground where Nathan had been walking. Peering down into it, they jumped back with shock as Nathan's head popped up.

"Aaaaahhhh!" they screamed in unison.

"It's okay!" replied Nathan. "The hole wasn't very deep! And look what I found down there…"

Nathan held up a small, shiny box that gleamed and sparkled, even in the gloomy rain.

"What is it?" Janine asked.

Just as she spoke, the box slipped from Nathan's fingers and landed on the wet grass. The lid flipped open and a twinkly swirl of light flew into the air. The children gasped in amazement, as a tiny figure materialised in front of them. A man, no more than five or six inches tall, hovered in the air before landing on a nearby sunflower. He had a bushy white beard and was wearing a pointed red hat.

"Ohhhh…" he groaned. "My aching back! I've been in that box for bloomin' years!"

Nathan, eyes and mouth wide with surprise, asked the little man who and what he was.

"I'm Eric!" he stated, puffing out his chest proudly. "Eric the Elf, young sir! You have freed me from a trap set for me a long time ago by a particularly grumpy wizard!"

"You're an elf?!" Nathan said. "That's incredible!"

The little elf looked flattered.

"You said it, young man!" he replied. "I am incredible. And seeing as how you've freed me from that box, and furthermore, seeing as how you seem to be a young man of exceedingly good taste, I will grant you three wishes!"

Barely pausing for thought, Nathan said, "I wish my family would disappear!" With a tinkling of bells, Janine, Christian and their parents promptly vanished. Nathan sat on the wet grass, not quite believing what had happened.

"Is… is that it?" he asked. "Are they r…really gone?"

Eric gestured around the garden. "Look around you !" he said. Certainly, Janine and Christian were no longer there. Eric leant forwards and prodded Nathan. "Listen, sonny, I'm a busy elf! What's your second wish?"

"I wish I was somewhere nice and hot, all by myself!" Nathan answered. And suddenly, he was alone on a beautiful beach, the blue sky arching high over his head and the sea glittering like polished diamonds and stretching away for ever.

"Wow!" Nathan said, getting to his feet and running across the hot sand. "This is brilliant, eh, Eric? Eric?" There was no answer. Nathan whirled around quickly, looking everywhere. "Eric?" he shouted again, but there was no reply, only the sound of the sea, lapping gently at the shore.

He ran around for what seemed like ages, but the empty beach seemed to have no end, and the tropical forest that bordered the beach looked a bit dark and scary.

Finally, hot, tired and more than a little worried, he flopped down on the sand and began to sob quietly. If only he could be back with all his family around him in that funny little bungalow on the edge of the wet and dreary seaside town!

"Well, I'm sure that can be arranged!" said a little voice at Nathan's side, making him jump. It was Eric. "You said you wanted to be alone, so I thought I'd give you a little time to yourself!"

"I want to go back and I want my family to be back with me!" Nathan said, breathlessly.

"And is that your third and final wish, then?" Eric asked. Nathan nodded his head vigorously.

"Oh, it is! It is!" he said.

"I'll see what I can do," said Eric.

Janine tugged at his arm and Nathan felt the rain against his face. "Come up out of that hole!" she said, as she and Christian peered down at him. Nathan climbed out of the damp hole and looked around, feeling very glad to be back. He could see his mum and dad inside the house and thought to himself that it was one of the nicest sights he had ever seen.

"Your brother and sister won't remember me!" Eric said, appearing in front of Nathan. "But I think you will, and you'll remember what you learnt today!"

"You bet!" Nathan said. "I'll never take my family for granted again! Even if they do bring me for a lovely week in a delightful town by the sea!"

And as Eric twinkled from sight, Nathan looked up at the grey sky, took his sister's hand, and ran inside laughing to join his family!

BARON BEEFBURGER

WRITTEN BY CANDY WALLACE

A very long time ago in a far off land, lived the evil Baron Beefburger. He had a twirly black moustache and a silly haircut that looked as though someone had put a pudding basin on his head and cut round it. He dressed in black and always had an evil sneer on his face.

The baron lived in a great castle and made his courtiers' lives an absolute misery. Not only was he always grumpy, but there was nothing he liked better than to hurl a custard pie in someone's face.

The castle cooks worked day and night cooking the Baron's favourite beefburgers and an endless supply of custard pies, while the castle laundry worked overtime cleaning all the custardy clothes.

In the castle lived the beautiful Princess Petunia and a knight called Sir Fightalot. Sir Fightalot was madly in love with the princess and she rather liked him too. But the evil baron wanted the princess for himself. So poor Sir Fightalot received more than his fair share of custard pies and never had a clean suit of armour to wear.

One day, while Sir Fightalot was out jousting, the baron went to see the princess. When she saw him coming she put a box over her head quickly in case he had a custard pie with him.

"Come, come, my dear," said the baron in an oily voice. "I only want to talk to you." The princess took the box off her head and sat down with her chin in her hands looking glum. "What do you want?" she said, sulkily.

"I'm having a little dinner party tomorrow evening…" he said. 'Just for two…" and he put his face close to hers with a horrible smile. "I'd advise you to come, or you might find a custard pie in your bed…"

When Sir Fightalot returned and found out what the baron had been up to, he was hopping mad. Something had to be done. He decided to go and see his wise and tubby friend, Friar Tuckshop.

"We've got to do something about him," said Sir Fightalot to his friend the friar. "He's after the princess and everyone in the castle is sick and tired of being covered in custard."

Friar Tuckshop looked thoughtful. "There's only one creature in the land more powerful than the baron," he said finally. "About 20 leagues away from here lives a dragon in a cave on a hillside. He's the only available monster for miles. What's more, he's not too keen on the baron. I remember a couple of years ago the baron sent the entire army to kill the dragon and make him into an umbrella stand for the Great Hall. They didn't succeed, of course, but it didn't make a very good impression on the dragon. I think he might help us."

The next morning, they set off to find the dragon. Sir Fightalot's knees were knocking the whole way and Friar

Tuckshop had to stop every now and then for a restoring snack. After some hours, walking over hill and dale, they arrived at the dragon's cave. It was set halfway up a sheer rock face and they could see the smoke from the dragon's nostrils curling up into the air outside the cave. Sir Fightalot looked at Friar Tuckshop and gulped.

"Are you sure he won't eat us?" he said.

"No, I'm not," Friar Tuckshop replied, "but it's too late to go back now!"

The two intrepid but trembling travellers climbed up to the mouth of the cave and peered in.

"Good afternoon," said the dragon. "Would you care for a cup of tea?"

Now it's a funny thing about dragons. People are very scared of them and run away. When they do go near one it's usually because they want to kill it and take it back to impress some princess or other, which means that dragons get rather lonely and fed up.

So the dragon was really pleased to see the nervous, but friendly, Sir Fightalot and Friar Tuckshop. They found themselves being entertained to a pot of tea and a plate of fairy cakes. Very relieved they hadn't been eaten after all, they explained (in between mouthfuls of cake) about the troublesome baron's latest tricks. Together with the dragon (whose name was Humphrey) they devised a clever plan…

That night, the baron sat at one end of his huge dinner table in the Great Hall and poor Princess Petunia sat at the other end looking bored. The baron, with a napkin around his neck, was tucking into a plate of his favourite beefburgers smothered in tomato sauce. A pile of custard pies lay on the table ready for anyone who dared to interrupt his romantic candlelit dinner with the princess.

"Bah!" he spluttered, suddenly. "These beefburgers are burnt!" He turned in fury to a trembling footman. "Bring the cook to me this minute!" and he threw a custard pie at the poor man as he sped out of the door.

Before you could say "knife and fork", the door to the Great Hall opened and in came — Humphrey the dragon! He was wearing a chef's hat and apron and wielding a giant wooden spoon. The baron was somewhat taken aback, but managed to shout:

"These beefburgers are burnt — you're fired!"

"No," replied the dragon. "You're fired," and he breathed on the baron's beefburgers. In seconds they were reduced to smouldering cinders. The princess began to think this wasn't going to be such a bad evening after all. The baron, meanwhile, was speechless with terror and held his napkin over his face.

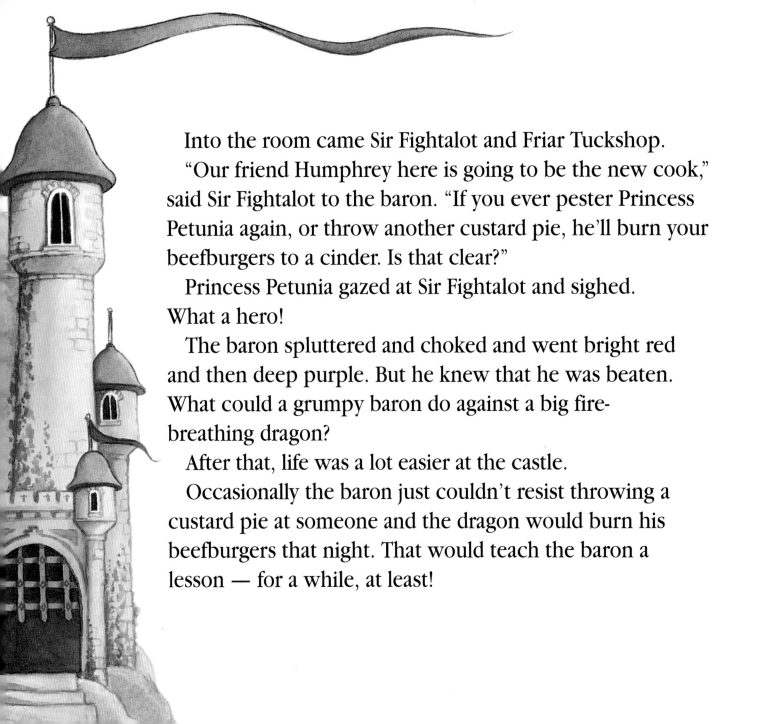

Into the room came Sir Fightalot and Friar Tuckshop.

"Our friend Humphrey here is going to be the new cook," said Sir Fightalot to the baron. "If you ever pester Princess Petunia again, or throw another custard pie, he'll burn your beefburgers to a cinder. Is that clear?"

Princess Petunia gazed at Sir Fightalot and sighed. What a hero!

The baron spluttered and choked and went bright red and then deep purple. But he knew that he was beaten. What could a grumpy baron do against a big fire-breathing dragon?

After that, life was a lot easier at the castle.

Occasionally the baron just couldn't resist throwing a custard pie at someone and the dragon would burn his beefburgers that night. That would teach the baron a lesson — for a while, at least!

The princess was so impressed with brave Sir Fightalot that she married him.

Meanwhile, Humphrey the dragon stayed on as the castle cook and was very happy. He loved cooking and, best of all, he wasn't lonely any more. He never did go back to his cave on the hillside. To thank him for taming the baron, the courtiers gave him a whole tower to himself and the run of the castle kitchen. Everyone agreed he made the best fairy cakes they had ever eaten and his fiery barbecues were the talk of the land. And if the baron fancied a custard pie — he had to make it himself!

BULKY THE GIANT

WRITTEN BY GEOFF COWAN

As giants go, Bulky was okay. He was what you might call a gentle giant. He was always polite to the local villagers. He did his very best not to upset them, which, being huge, wasn't easy.

Take Bulky's feet, for instance. His shoes seemed like boats to the villagers. Even if Bulky tiptoed past their homes, he still made the ground tremble. The startled folk fell out of bed, kitchen crockery rattled and furniture bounced about.

The villagers complained to Bulky. They only dared to because he was so nice and kind. He even said sorry and promised to creep around more carefully than before.

"I should think so," said the villagers, impatiently.

Then there was his sneezing. Now everyone sneezes from time to time, and giants are no different. But when Bulky sneezed he sent such a blast of air howling across the valley, the villagers had to rush indoors for fear of being blown away!

They complained to Bulky about that as well. The giant promised he would sneeze into his hanky, which, after all, is only the polite thing to do. But sometimes a sneeze came upon him all of a sudden, before he could do anything about it.

One complaint followed another. Eventually the villagers decided life would be much more comfortable without a giant living on their doorstep. So they sent for Spellbound the Wizard and asked him if he could shrink Bulky down to normal human size. Bulky agreed to the plan at once, proving what a big-hearted giant he was!

"Abracadabra, pots, pans and sink,
A wave of my wand will make Bulky shrink!"
As Spellbound chanted the rhyme he gave his wand a few extra waves for luck. Sometimes, his spells needed it!

All at once, a silvery mist appeared, hiding Bulky from sight. When it cleared, the delighted villagers saw that Bulky was just the same size as them!

For a while everyone lived peacefully. Bulky moved in with a kind family who looked after him very well, and he began to enjoy life at his new size.

Now life's full of little surprises, but the surprise that arrived from beyond the mountains surrounding the villagers' valley was big as in giant; the walking, talking type, just like Bulky used to be!

Heavyhand was short-tempered and always wanted to get his own way. The villagers didn't know this at first. But they soon found out. When Heavyhand lay down for a snooze in a lush, green meadow, sending sheep scattering, the villagers complained, just as they had to Bulky.

But Heavyhand roared angrily at them and warned that if he wasn't left in peace, he would flatten every home in the village! Then he banged his fist mightily on the ground. The frightened villagers jumped into the air, and scattered in all directions.

"Clear off!" he bellowed. "I like this valley and I'm here to stay!"

From that day on, Heavyhand stomped about wherever he pleased, flattening crops, and knocking down trees. When he lay down for a rest, he always slipped off his boots and used them as a pillow. He had horribly smelly feet, and the rotten pong wafted through the valley, sending everyone indoors, rushing to shut their doors and windows. And when he slept, he snored louder than thunder. The villagers huddled in their homes, holding their heads and wishing Heavyhand would go away. But he wouldn't.

It wasn't long before they began to wish something else.

"If only Bulky were still big, he'd soon see off Heavyhand!" sighed one.

"It's our own silly fault," agreed a second.

"We shouldn't have been so selfish," said a third. "Bulky was such a thoughtful, kind and good-tempered giant. He never did anyone any harm!"

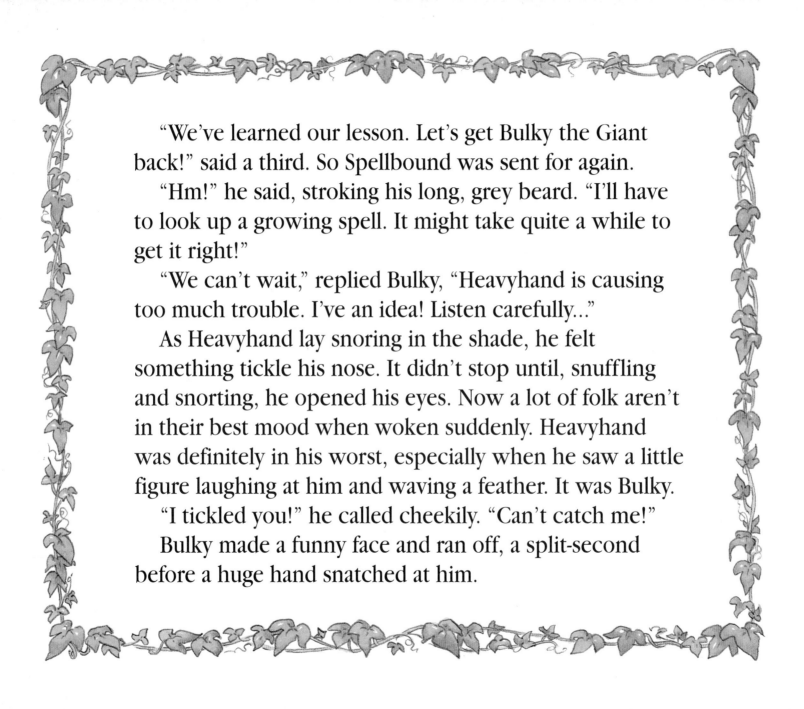

"We've learned our lesson. Let's get Bulky the Giant back!" said a third. So Spellbound was sent for again.

"Hm!" he said, stroking his long, grey beard. "I'll have to look up a growing spell. It might take quite a while to get it right!"

"We can't wait," replied Bulky, "Heavyhand is causing too much trouble. I've an idea! Listen carefully..."

As Heavyhand lay snoring in the shade, he felt something tickle his nose. It didn't stop until, snuffling and snorting, he opened his eyes. Now a lot of folk aren't in their best mood when woken suddenly. Heavyhand was definitely in his worst, especially when he saw a little figure laughing at him and waving a feather. It was Bulky.

"I tickled you!" he called cheekily. "Can't catch me!"

Bulky made a funny face and ran off, a split-second before a huge hand snatched at him.

Bulky jumped onto a horse he'd left nearby, and galloped towards the mountains, while a furious Heavyhand reached for his boots. But some of the villagers had tied the laces together and by the time Heavyhand had unknotted them, Bulky had reached the mouth of an enormous cave.

He didn't try to hide, but waited till Heavyhand had seen him before disappearing inside, with Heavyhand in hot pursuit! Bulky had found the cave long ago, during his days as a giant. He knew another way out, if you were small enough. Now, of course, he was! Bulky scrambled out into the fresh air.

The villagers were ready for their part of the plan!

As Bulky rode clear, they pushed against a rock high above the cave mouth, heaving and shoving until they set it rolling down the mountain, loosening others as it went, until an avalanche fell across the front of the cave. Heavyhand had no time to escape.

"He's trapped inside!" cried the villagers.

But not for long!

How the mountain trembled as Heavyhand raged and cursed, as he began to dig himself out. He worked all day and night. So did Spellbound, until at last his spell was ready. The wizard's wand whirled and he muttered strange magic words. A dazzling arc of stars appeared around Bulky who began to grow and grow, just as Heavyhand came bursting from the cave.

Imagine his surprise when he saw Bulky standing a good head and broad shoulders above him. Even for a giant, Bulky was big.

"Go and find your own valley. This one's mine!" roared Bulky, raising his voice for the first time in his life.

None of the villagers minded one bit. They were only too pleased to see good old Bulky back to normal. Heavyhand took off nervously across the mountains without looking back.

"We promise never to complain again, Bulky," the thankful villagers told him. "We know we made a big mistake before!"

"More like a giant one!" someone joked and everyone laughed, though Bulky took care not to laugh too loudly!

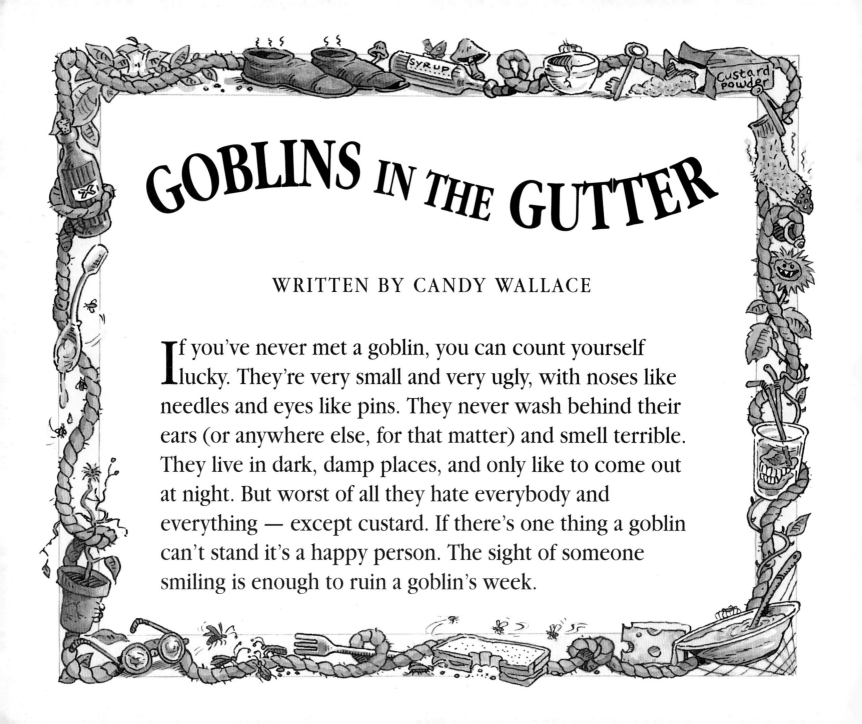

GOBLINS IN THE GUTTER

WRITTEN BY CANDY WALLACE

If you've never met a goblin, you can count yourself lucky. They're very small and very ugly, with noses like needles and eyes like pins. They never wash behind their ears (or anywhere else, for that matter) and smell terrible. They live in dark, damp places, and only like to come out at night. But worst of all they hate everybody and everything — except custard. If there's one thing a goblin can't stand it's a happy person. The sight of someone smiling is enough to ruin a goblin's week.

There was once a little girl called Poppy who was always happy. She had a nice mum and dad and an older brother called Fred. Now if you've got an older brother, you probably think he's a pain in the neck. But Poppy thought Fred was the best thing since beefburgers.

"I'm really lucky to have a brother like him," she would say to her friends.

Poppy thought school was absolutely brilliant, too. There was nothing she liked more than two pages of sums to do — unless it was three pages of sums. Everybody else thought Miss Crochet the teacher was horrible and grumpy and made them work too hard. They put chewing gum on her chair and daddy-long-legs in her desk to make her screech. But Poppy thought she was funny and laughed at her.

Outside Poppy's house in Acacia Avenue there was a drain in the road. If you looked down it all you could see was dirty water at the bottom. It was dark and smelly and full of old lolly sticks, dead leaves and spiders. There were goblins living in that drain. You couldn't see them, but if you knelt down and put your ear to the ground you might have heard them arguing. Goblins are always arguing and fighting.

They had moved there when Chestnut Tree Close was dug up to lay new water pipes. They hadn't minded the noisy road drills. But laughing workmen who sang loud songs and told jokes were more than a goblin could stomach. So, at dead of night, they had packed up and made their way to Acacia Avenue, and the drain outside Poppy's house.

They soon realised this was a big mistake.

"It makes me feel sick," said Gruel, the oldest, grumpiest goblin, "every time I see Whatshername skipping along to school with a big smile on her face. She should be arrested for humming without due care and attention."

"Well I think we should sort her out," said a fat goblin called Squelch, who thought all children should be made into savoury pies. "If we can't wipe that smile off her face, I'm a pixie."

The next morning, two goblins popped their heads through the grille of the drain. Their mean little eyes darted about to make sure no one was around. They jumped out holding a length of dirty old string, tied one end to the drain and tiptoed across the pavement to tie the other end to the hedge outside Poppy's house.

"There's nothing like a couple of grazed knees to make children cry!" sniggered one. "Let's hope she enjoys the trip!" giggled the other and they jumped back inside the drain to wait and listen.

Sure enough, a few minutes later there was a cry and a commotion. Gleefully the goblins peeped out to survey their handiwork. But it wasn't Poppy they saw on the pavement — it was an old man, sitting with arms and legs waving in the air!

"Oh dear, oh dear!" said the old man. "Whatever happened? Thank goodness nothing's broken. That could have been a nasty fall!"

Poppy's mum and dad rushed out of the house to help him. So did Mr Entwhistle from across the road and Mrs Ramsbottom from number 67 .

"Are you all right, dear?" asked Poppy's mum, who was very worried about the old man. "Come on in and have a nice cup of tea. What horrid children would tie string across the path like that! Just wait till I catch them!"

"When you've had a nice cuppa I'll take you home," said Mrs Ramsbottom, anxiously.

"Thank you so much!" replied the old man, as they helped him out of the hedge. "Do you know, I've lived in this street for two years and no one has ever spoken to me before!" They all went into Poppy's house. "Well you can come round for tea any time, Mr — er —."

"Brown. Ernest Brown," said the old man, and smiled to himself happily.

"Rats!" hissed Spodworthy, Goblin-in-Chief, to Gruel. "We got the wrong person! We'd better get it right next time! All we've done is make someone else happy too!"

That night, Squelch crept along the drains underground up the pipes and through the plughole into the kitchen sink in Poppy's house. There on the table was her lunchbox for school, which Poppy's mum always packed the night before. He scurried to the rubbish bin and picked out a horrible smelly half-eaten fish. Then he opened her lunch box, took out all the cheese from the sandwiches and put the fish in instead! He threw the cheese in the bin, and put Poppy's chocolate cake in his pocket for later!

"If that doesn't make her cry at school today, I don't know what will!" he smirked, and dived back down the plughole. Squelch couldn't think of anything worse than going without your lunch…

Poppy was none the wiser. In the morning she walked out of the garden gate holding her lunchbox and humming a tune. Before long, she noticed a little cat following her, jumping up at the lunchbox and swiping it with her paw.

"Hello pussycat!" said Poppy, bending down to stroke her. "Oh dear, you look very thin and your fur is all matted and dull. Haven't you got a home?"

The little cat gave a feeble miaow and sniffed and pawed at her lunch box.

"You can have a sandwich if you like," said Poppy, and opened up her box. When she saw the fish sandwiches, she laughed. "Poor Mum must have been a bit muddled last night!" she said. "Come on, pussycat. Fred's always wanted a cat and you need someone to look after you."

Poppy picked up the cat and took her home. Fred was thrilled.

The goblins watched as Fred and Poppy fed the cat and played with her in the front garden. Spodworthy was beside himself with fury.

"Fools! Imbeciles! You've managed to turn one happy child and one miserable cat into two horribly happy children and one disgustingly happy cat!" he screamed at the other goblins.

That night, the goblins held a special committee meeting. They argued and shouted and jumped up and down. They boxed each others ears. Spodworthy stamped on Squelch's foot. Finally they came to a decision.

In the morning, Poppy kissed the cat (newly named Tiddles) and waved to Mr Brown. She skipped along the pavement, past the dark, silent drain.

The goblins had gone.

WONDERWHISKERS

WRITTEN BY GEOFF COWAN

Down among the plants and shrubs, in many a garden, you may come across a little painted stone figure with a bushy white beard and red, pointed hat. Often as not, he's sitting on a toadstool or fishing with a tiny rod. These little folk are, of course, garden gnomes. If you've seen one, then you'll know what a real gnome looks like.

Well, Wonderwhiskers was no different, except for his beard. It was the thickest, strongest and longest you could imagine. In fact, it was so long that Wonderwhiskers had

to part it down the middle and, with the help of other gnomes, roll it up into two bundles which he carried on his back.

Any sensible gnome would have cut such a beard and, in the early days, Wonderwhiskers had tried to. But by next day, it had always grown longer than before.

"Amazing!" he'd gasp, as he stared at his beard in the mirror. So he decided he'd just have to live with it.

Besides, Wonderwhiskers was very proud of his beard. It had made him famous! The other gnomes treated him with the greatest respect, and would do anything he asked them. There wasn't a gnome in the land who hadn't invited him home for a slap-up meal. Oh, yes! Wonderwhiskers was definitely a V.I.G., a Very Important Gnome. But it had not always been like that…

There was a time when Wonderwhiskers had been just

your average common-or-garden gnome, by the name of Norman. He had lived in a snug underground home beneath an old storm-struck tree, deep in the heart of the forest. Norman and his gnome neighbours would go in search of tiny treasures to decorate their home, such as shiny pebbles, a lucky four-leaved clover or even a fluffy feather, dropped by one of their bird friends.

That, however, was before Norman's beard had begun to grow and grow. Before long it became a bit of a nuisance. The end would blow into Norman's face so that he couldn't see where he was going. Once, Norman had walked straight into his friend Tiggletum who dropped a sackful of forest treasures on his toe. Even after Norman began to roll up his beard, it sometimes came loose and dragged along the ground, like the time when his cousin Lightstep tripped on it and went flying into a puddle.

Yet, every night before he went to bed, Norman always washed and brushed his beard before measuring it to see just how much longer it had grown. Such a big, bushy beard made him feel special.

"The bigger his beard, the bigger Norman's head!" others began to utter with just a teensy-weensy hint of jealousy as word spread of his incredible beard, and visitors came from far and wide to see it.

Then, one day, some unbelievable news caused the gnomes to chatter excitedly.

"King Cracklecorn's coming! Imagine! The King of the Gnomes visiting us!" cried Norman's neighbours.

"He must have heard about my beard, too," said Norman proudly.

"Don't flatter yourself," replied Tiggletum. "He's coming because I wrote to him!"

"You what?!" gasped Norman.

"Didn't I tell you?" continued Tiggletum, looking oh-so-smug. "I found the rarest treasure of all. The king's sure to reward me!"

"What is it, this treasure?" asked Norman.

"It's the place where the rainbow ends," announced Tiggletum. "Every gnome knows it's a magical place, where you'll find a pot of gold!"

"Why didn't you bring the gold back with you?" asked another gnome, called Bizzybonce.

Tiggletum shuffled his feet and looked awkward. "Well, I think I've found the rainbow's end," he explained. "One sunny afternoon last week I went out for a walk, but it began to rain. A rainbow appeared. I saw one end dip towards a clearing. I ran all the way there but, by the time I arrived, the rain had stopped so the rainbow vanished. But I should be able to find the spot again!"

"I hope so!" frowned Lightfoot. "Fancy inviting the king without being sure!"

It was too late for Tiggletum to start worrying now. Before they knew it the king was on the doorstep and they all set off to find the rainbow's end. By the time they had covered half the forest and walked in circles for a few hours, everyone was feeling grumpy, especially the king.

To make matters worse, it began to rain. No sun, mind you; just rain, rain and more rain. As they hurried back to their homes, they decided to take the short cut beside the brook. But it had swollen to a fast-flowing stream and that's when the king had an accident. He slipped, fell in and was nearly washed away.

"Someone fetch a rope!" yelled Tiggletum, as King Cracklecorn clung to a piece of driftwood that, for a lucky moment, had jammed between two rocks amid the rapids.

"We don't have a rope! We don't have anything that can save him!" cried Bizzybonce.

"Oh, yes we have!" replied Norman. He unrolled his beard which he'd kept neatly behind his back as usual. Next moment, he threw the end to the king who managed to grasp it.

"Hold on, your Majesty!" called Norman. Turning to the others, he said, "Hurry! Help me pull him towards us!"

Inch by inch, through the surging water, the King of the Gnomes was pulled closer. Norman closed his eyes, bit his lip and never uttered a sound, although it must have been very painful. After all, imagine how hard his beard was being tugged! Ouch!

But, at last, helping hands lifted the weary king clear and he sat puffing on the riverbank. Soaked but safe, he turned to Norman.

"I hereby name you Wonderwhiskers," he said thankfully, "and grant you the title of S.M.I.G!"

"Second Most Important Gnome," whispered
Tiggletum to the others in amazement. "That means only
the king is more important than Norman, I mean
Wonderwhiskers, now!"
They all thought he had been incredibly brave and
clever. As they went to congratulate him, they slipped on
his dripping beard, toppled into each other and landed in
a happy heap. Everyone laughed, including the king.
And from that day on, the invitations poured through
Wonderwhiskers' letterbox. He spent his time enjoying
one visit after another, to tell his famous story or show off
his fabulous beard. His admiring hosts did everything they
could to make such a noble gnome feel comfortable.
As Wonderwhiskers often joked to himself, it was just
like home from home … or gnome from gnome!

MONSTER MAYHEM

WRITTEN BY CLAIRE STEEDEN

In a group of caves, in the heart of a dark, dark forest, there once lived a collection of marvellous monsters. In one of the caves lived Rugged Red. He was terribly vain and spent nearly all day long looking at himself in the mirror. In fact, he did not have just one mirror, but hundreds of them. So wherever he turned he could see his reflection. He loved his deep ruby red colour and told himself often how marvellous he looked. He was particularly proud of the smooth red spikes that stuck out all over his body.

Paul Gamble.

Every day he would sit in his cave, turning his head this way and that, admiring his reflection.

"Oh, you are so handsome," he would say to himself.

He would try all different sorts of hair styles and pull a number of faces to see which expressions made him look his best.

Now, this in itself was bad enough, but all of Rugged's neighbours were exactly the same, if not worse. They all thought that they were the most handsome or beautiful monster in the world. As you can imagine, they were always arguing about who was the loveliest colour or who had the most attractive hairstyle..

Perfect Purple thought that her purple curls were absolutely fabulous. Brilliant Blue, with his shiny scales, said that he was the most breathtaking monster of all. While Awesome Orange argued that his ringlets were the most remarkable of all.

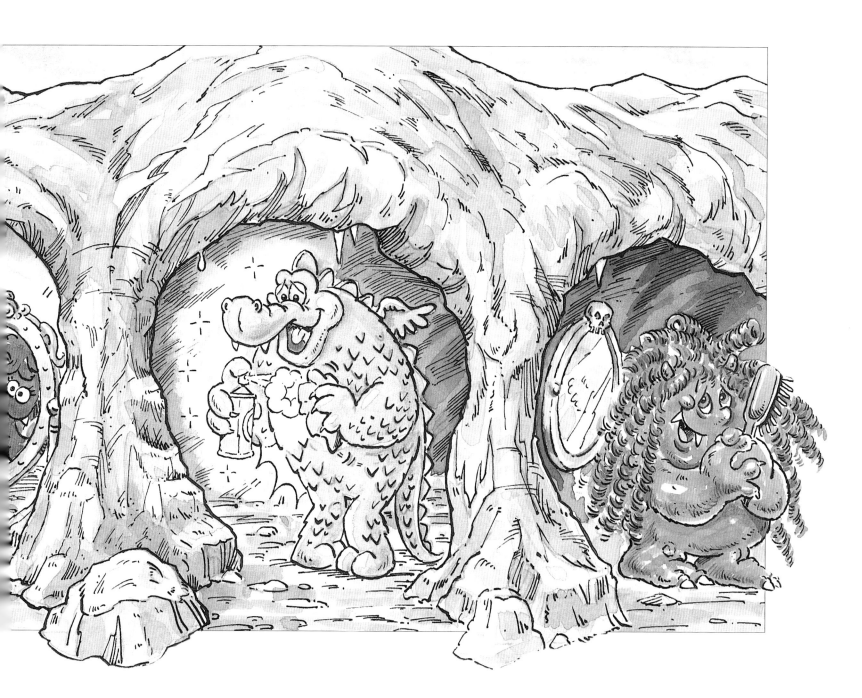

Now, one day, Gorgeous Green, who was the Great Governor of the monsters, got fed up with listening to all the arguing and fighting, so she thought of a cunning plan to put a stop to it, once and for all. She decided to give a huge party and invite all the monsters. She made a long list and sent out posh invitations. Each one matched the colour of the monster she was inviting.

All the monsters were very excited. Wherever you went all you could hear were monsters arguing about who would look the best at the party. Even a few monsters that were not usually as vain as the others fell out with their friends.

The whole place buzzed with excitement. The hairdressers were busy. The Spike Specialists were fully booked. The Scale Scrapers were overrun with customers, not to mention the Claw Clippers and Fang Filers.

The air was filled with talk about colour and style, and size and shape — what a hullabaloo. The monsters argued and preened and shouted and screamed until the noise was unbearable.

When it was nearly time for the party to start the monsters began to queue outside the gates of Gorgeous Green's garden. Together they formed a rainbow of colours — red, yellow, pink, green, orange, purple and blue. It was a splendid sight to see them all standing next to each other.

At two o'clock the gates were opened and the monsters filed in. As they entered they were each given a sparkling drink which tasted very unusual. It kept changing colour, and tiny coloured bubbles rose from the top.

Gorgeous Green had decorated her garden with balloons and streamers, and lots and lots of mirrors.

Finally, all the monsters arrived and the party got underway.
There were long tables full of scrummy things to eat and
a big bowl of punch, which looked delicious.

Gorgeous Green had organised party
games and had hired a band to play
all their favourite monster music.

It had all the ingredients of a perfect party, except for one thing. None of the monsters were interested in the food, the party games or the music. They were all much too busy looking at their reflections and arguing about who was the nicest colour.

Gorgeous Green had known that this would happen. She knew how unfriendly and vain all the monsters were and she was tired of seeing everyone so miserable. The monsters had forgotten how to have fun.

She stood on a platform and signalled to the band to stop playing. Then she spoke to the monsters.

"I have invited you all to my party for a special reason. I have been watching and listening to you all for a long time. It makes me sad to see you all fighting, especially when there is no reason to. You are all wonderful, and nobody is a nicer colour than anyone else."

With this all the monsters started talking at once. How could she say such a thing? It was ridiculous!

"Please listen. I've invited you all here to have fun and enjoy yourselves, but you are all too busy arguing. Well, I knew that talking to you all wouldn't stop you from quarrelling, so I asked Wizzle the Wizard to make me a magic potion. As you came in you all drank a glass of his potion, and I'm glad to see that it has started to work. Go and look at yourselves in the mirrors."

With that, all the monsters turned to look at their reflections, and guess what had happened! Instead of seeing a blue monster, or yellow monster in the mirror, they were grey. Every single monster had turned grey! They gasped and turned to Gorgeous Green in astonishment.

"I thought that if everyone looked the same, there would be nothing more to argue about.Now you can enjoy the party and have fun with your friends."

The monsters looked down at themselves and then at each other. One by one they realised how silly they had been. All that time they had wasted when they could have been having fun.

The band started to play and Gorgeous Green, who was also grey by now, organised lots of games to play. All the monsters had a wonderful afternoon. None of them could remember when they had had such a good time. They played, and danced and ate and laughed and sang

Gorgeous Green felt very happy. Her plan had worked. The monsters had stopped arguing at last.

Again she stood up to speak to them.

"This afternoon I think you've learnt a very important lesson. Now you can see that being a different colour doesn't matter. We are all friends because we like each other and nobody is better than anyone else. Since you have learnt your lesson, I think it's time to change back to our original colours. If you each have a glass of the punch on this table, you will turn back to the colour you were."

Everyone drank the punch and started to change back slowly. But this time they did not argue. They carried on with the party late into the night. Nobody wanted to go home, they all wanted to stay and have fun with all their new found friends!

THE TOOTH FAIRY

WRITTEN BY CANDY WALLACE

It all began when Thomas Timpson went to tea with his Grandma. Thomas's Grandma made very nice teas — well, almost! She made little squidgy sandwiches and wibbly-wobbly green jellies and strawberry milkshakes so frothy you got pink bubbles on the end of your nose. And she made rock cakes. Grandma's rock cakes were like — um— rocks. If you dropped one, Grandma's best china shook and rattled on the sideboard and her cat, Tibbles, ran in terror to hide under the sofa.

One day, when Thomas Timpson went to tea and bit into one of Grandma's rock cakes, his wobbly tooth came out and dropped onto his plate with a clink.

"Lucky Thomas!" said Grandma, "Let me put that tooth in a napkin for you. You must take it home and put it under your pillow for the Tooth Fairy!"

When Grandma disappeared into the kitchen, Thomas quickly popped the rest of his rock cake in the plant pot where Grandma's aspidistra grew. That's where he always put his rock cakes.

Thomas wasn't too sure about this Tooth Fairy business, but he was prepared to give it a try. So that night he put his tooth under his pillow and went to sleep.

The next morning, Thomas was amazed to find that his tooth had gone — and there was a shiny new coin lying in its place!

Thomas couldn't understand why anybody would want his old tooth, but he was very glad to have the coin. When he emptied his money-box he discovered there was nearly enough now to buy a new football!

The next week, to his delight, Thomas found that he had another wobbly tooth. He wiggled and jiggled it, but it just wouldn't budge.

"Mum," said Thomas, "please can I go to tea with Grandma?"

Grandma was pleased to see Thomas again. "I've made you some of your favourite rock cakes!" she said.

"What does the Tooth Fairy do with children's teeth, Grandma?" said Thomas, munching on a cheese and cucumber sandwich.

"You'll have to ask the Tooth Fairy," Grandma chuckled and went to get a fresh batch of rock cakes out of the oven.

"Now you tuck into those dear," said Grandma, "while I water my aspidistra, it's not looking at all well nowadays…"

Thomas closed his eyes tight and bit bravely into a cake. Hey, presto! Out came the tooth!

That night, Thomas didn't put the tooth under his pillow but instead decided to take Grandma's advice. He wrote a note which said:

"Dear Tooth Fairy, I do have a tooth for you but it's hidden. Wake me up and I'll tell you where it is. What do you want it for? Love Thomas."

And he settled down and went to sleep.

He was in the middle of a horrible dream where a giant rock cake with big teeth was trying to eat him when he suddenly woke up. He was amazed to see a tiny creature on his pillow, with miniature spectacles on her nose, reading his note and tutting to herself.

Thomas rubbed his eyes to make sure he wasn't still dreaming.

"Excuse me," he said, "are you the Tooth Fairy?"

"Yes I am, and after tonight I'm going to ask for a transfer to Dingly Dell duty. Dancing round a couple of toadstools is going to be a piece of cake after this job."

"I'll tell you where my tooth is if you tell me what you're going to use it for," said Thomas firmly.

"In my day children kept quiet and did as they were told," said the fairy, looking very cross. She put her spectacles away in a tiny pocket and folded her arms. "All right, it's a deal."

Thomas took his tooth from his bedside drawer and gave it to the fairy.

"But I don't have time to explain," she said. "You'll have to come and see for yourself."

Thomas was thrilled. "Will you whisk me off to Fairyland with a magic wand?" he asked excitedly, remembering the school play. Janice Potts had a wand to go with her fairy costume made out of a stick with a silver star on the end.

"You're a bit behind the times," sniffed the fairy, taking out a tiny remote control that sparkled in the moonlight. She pointed it at Thomas and pressed the button…

"WOW!" Thomas was standing in a vast room that sparkled and shone, as though covered with silvery cobwebs. In the middle of the room was a huge machine with a giant funnel at the top and a moving conveyor belt beneath. At the top of the funnel a big swinging bucket was filling up and emptying its cargo into the funnel. From the other end came a fine, sparkly powder that reflected all the colours of the rainbow. It flowed like a river along the conveyor belt to where it was dropped into little sacks and sealed.

Hundreds of fairies were busy everywhere, scurrying away with the sacks to load them onto little trollies, counting and making notes, bringing more supplies for the funnel. Dozens of little lights flashed on and off.

"See that funnel?" said the Tooth Fairy. "That's where your tooth will go. All the little teeth are dropped into there and what comes out the other end is magic powder. It's the secret ingredient in lots of our spells. We used pearls in the old days, but they're rather difficult to get hold of now."

mind the steps

"So now you use teeth!" exclaimed Thomas.

"Teeth are very valuable to us fairies," said the Tooth Fairy. "That's why we always pay you."

Thomas gazed in amazement at the sparkling scene. Magic powder hung in the air all around. When he looked down at his hand, it glittered in the silvery light.

"I have to take tonight's teeth to the stores," said the fairy, "and you must go back before morning. But since you're here, I'll grant you three wishes. We *had* cut wishes down to two but we've got a special offer on at the moment."

Thomas could hardly believe his ears. He closed his eyes and took a deep breath.

"I wish that I could buy my new football … and I wish that Grandma's rock cakes were light and fluffy … and I wish that her aspidistra would get better…"

Before he could finish speaking, the fairy factory had vanished. He was lying in his bed with the sun shining through his window. Feeling under the pillow, he felt a coin! Thomas rushed to his piggy bank and shook out all the money. He counted carefully. Yes! There was enough for the new football!

He took it round to Grandma's the following week when he went for tea. "Very nice, dear," said Grandma, as she brought in some delicious-smelling rock cakes fresh from the oven. Thomas sank his teeth into one and took a big bite. It was soft and crumbly, and full of big, juicy currants.

"These are great, Grandma!" he said in a mumbly sort of way because his mouth was full.

"Thank you, dear. It's a new recipe. Now you tuck in while I water my aspidistra — it's coming on a treat."

MAGIC MIX-UP!

WRITTEN BY CLAIRE STEEDEN

One sunny morning Wanda the Witch woke up, rubbed her eyes and climbed out of her rather saggy bed. She put on her favourite black dress with purple stars. It was quite tatty as she wore it every day. She tied a belt round her plump belly and pulled on her shoes with curly wurly toes. Then she pushed her hair up into her pointy hat as it was so tangled she could not get a brush through it. She looked in the mirror and laughed.

"What a mess. Still, I've no time to waste on myself."

Wanda was always busy doing spells for her friends.
Her 'rock into enormous sticky chocolate pudding'
spell was frequently in demand. However, her
wand had never been quite the same
since it had fallen into her cauldron
and her spells often got in a muddle.

This morning Wanda had an important spell to do. Harriet the Hedgehog was having a birthday party for her son Harry that afternoon, and Wanda was making a special cake. She lifted her enormous book of spells off the shelf, popped her glasses on her long nose and peered at the first page.

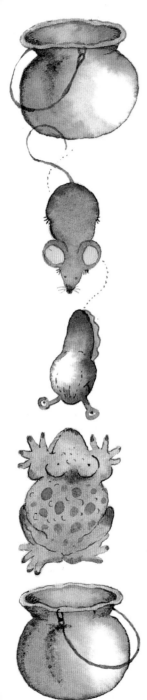

"Bestest birthday cakes," she read out, "page seventy-three."

She turned the pages filled with magic. "Let's see what we need. One large frog, got that, a cup of rats' tails, got that, some slimy slugs, got them, and a pretty, scented flower for decoration. Bother, I haven't got one of those. Mix together, throw mixture into the air, wave your wand and say the magic words:

'Up in the air, twist and shake,
Make me the bestest birthday cake.'

Well that sounds simple. I just need to go and pick a flower." Wanda put on her shawl and bustled down the garden path and into the forest, where she found a small bush with the prettiest flowers. Wanda bent down to pick one, held it under her nose to sniff and tucked it into her pocket.

As she stood up she heard someone humming close by. Wanda crept behind a huge oak tree. Peeping out, she saw the beautiful Princess Primula, who had long golden curly hair, big brown eyes, dainty little hands and a gorgeous sparkly pink gown. Wanda looked down at herself and realised how shabby and ugly she was. At that moment Princess Primula rounded the tree and came face to face with Wanda. The princess let out an almighty scream and ran away as fast as she could.

"I must have really scared her. She is so beautiful and I'm so ugly." A tear rolled down Wanda's cheek. Then she had an idea. "I'm always doing magic for other people. I should do some for myself. I'll go home and make myself as beautiful as the princess."

Picking up her skirt she ran as fast as her short fat legs could carry her. Wanda flicked through her book of spells and found a spell to make lovely long hair. She took off her hat, picked up her wand and said the magic words:

"Take away this tangled mess, and in its place
put hair. As long and fine as it can be,
to make me look most fair."
But when she felt her head, instead of soft silky
hair, she felt something smooth and shiny. She was
completely bald!

"Oh bother," she cried. "This stupid wand. I'll
have to buy a new one the next time I go to
Witchways. Oh well, I'll come back to my hair later.
I think I'll try making my hands and feet smaller."
Wanda found the right spell and read it out carefully.
"My hands and feet are far too big,
I'd like them to be tiny.
With skin as soft as purest silk,
And nails all long and shiny."
But, oh dear, when Wanda held out her arms
there at the end were two dainty little feet. When
she stuck out her legs there were two pretty
hands on the end of each. "Drat and blast. What a
muddle. Oh well, I'll sort them out later."

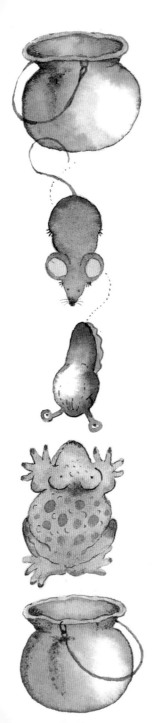

Wanda decided to try to make her nose and chin less pointed. She read out the spell:

"Go away you pointy nose, and you pointy chin.
Instead be nice and rounded, pretty, small and trim."

She waved her wand above her head and hoped the spell had worked. But, oh dear, guess what happened. A very pretty little nose appeared, but not where a nose should be. It was on her chin, which was now much smaller.

"I'm really getting in a muddle. I'll try one more time, then I'd better sort out all those mixed-up spells. I think I'll try a spell to make me thinner."

"Bulges on my belly, bulges on my thighs.
Go away and don't come back, please be a smaller size."

With a wave of her wand she was instantly so thin that her dress fell off her shoulders and onto the floor. Wanda was left standing in the kitchen in just her underwear!

At that moment Harriet the Hedgehog knocked at the door and came in. She took one look at Wanda and burst into a fit of giggles. "What on earth are you doing?"

"I was trying to make myself beautiful," replied Wanda.

"Well, it looks like things have gone a bit wrong. Go and look at yourself in the mirror," giggled Harriet.

Wanda stood in front of her mirror and started to laugh.

"Oh dear, this really isn't quite what I had in mind. What a muddle," said Wanda.

"Why do you want to look beautiful?" asked Harriet. Wanda explained what had happened in the forest.

"Well, I don't know why you're making such a fuss. Although Princess Primula is beautiful on the outside, she's horrible inside. She's mean and selfish and nobody likes her," explained Harriet. "You may not be beautiful but you are kind and helpful and everybody loves you."

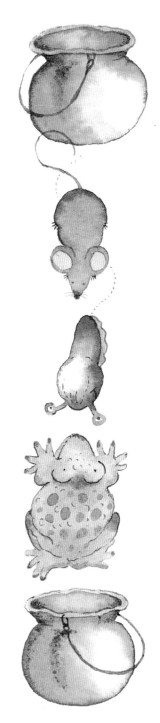

Bestest Birthday cakes

Ingredients:
1 large frog
Some Slimy Slugs
1 Scented Flower

1. Mix together.
2. Throw mixture Into the air.
3. Wave Your Wand.

73

Say magic words—
"Up in the air, twist and shake,
Make me the bestest birthday cake."

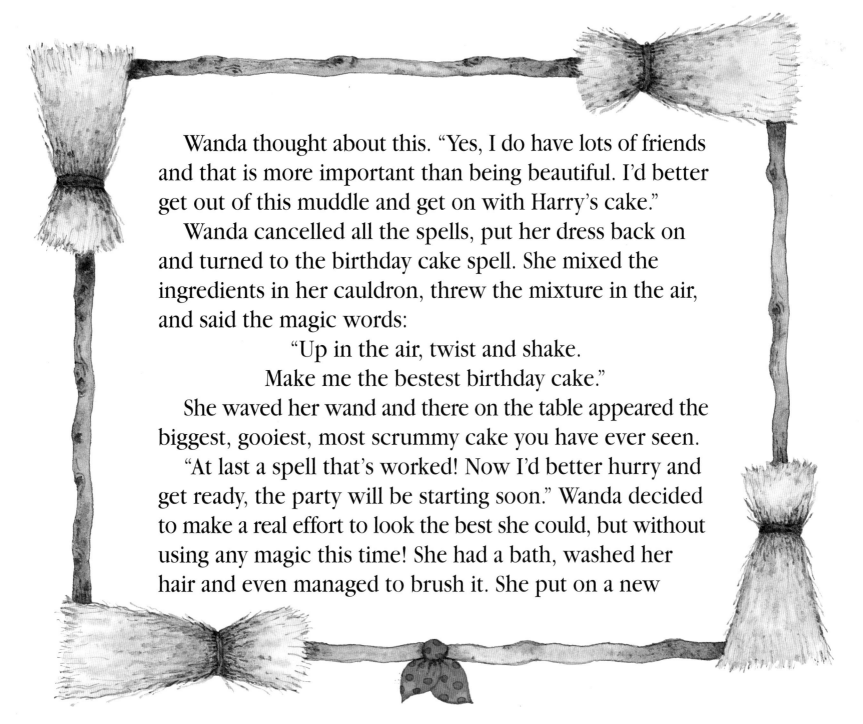

Wanda thought about this. "Yes, I do have lots of friends and that is more important than being beautiful. I'd better get out of this muddle and get on with Harry's cake."

Wanda cancelled all the spells, put her dress back on and turned to the birthday cake spell. She mixed the ingredients in her cauldron, threw the mixture in the air, and said the magic words:

"Up in the air, twist and shake.
Make me the bestest birthday cake."

She waved her wand and there on the table appeared the biggest, gooiest, most scrummy cake you have ever seen.

"At last a spell that's worked! Now I'd better hurry and get ready, the party will be starting soon." Wanda decided to make a real effort to look the best she could, but without using any magic this time! She had a bath, washed her hair and even managed to brush it. She put on a new

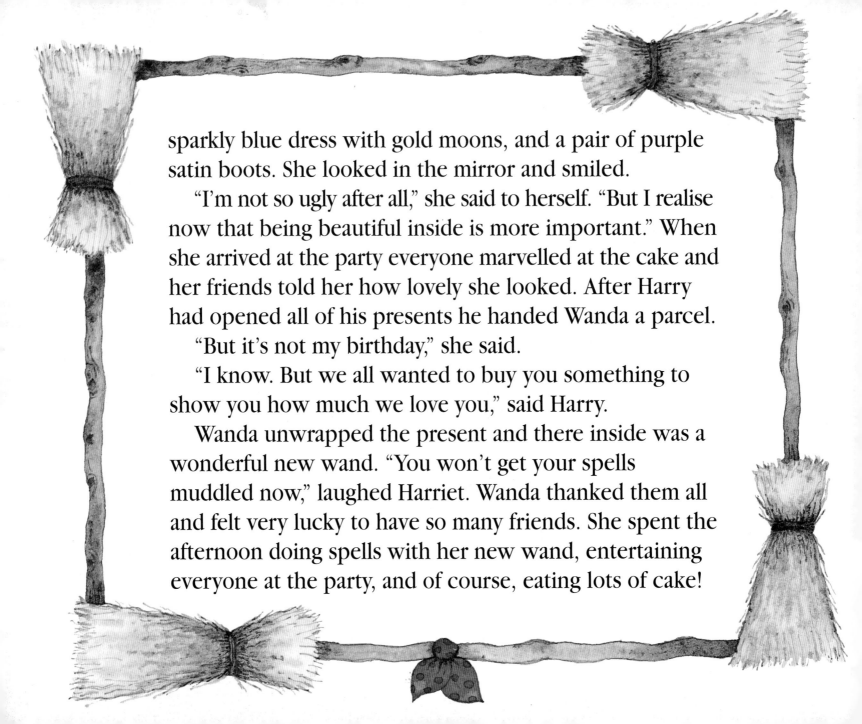

sparkly blue dress with gold moons, and a pair of purple satin boots. She looked in the mirror and smiled.

"I'm not so ugly after all," she said to herself. "But I realise now that being beautiful inside is more important." When she arrived at the party everyone marvelled at the cake and her friends told her how lovely she looked. After Harry had opened all of his presents he handed Wanda a parcel.

"But it's not my birthday," she said.

"I know. But we all wanted to buy you something to show you how much we love you," said Harry.

Wanda unwrapped the present and there inside was a wonderful new wand. "You won't get your spells muddled now," laughed Harriet. Wanda thanked them all and felt very lucky to have so many friends. She spent the afternoon doing spells with her new wand, entertaining everyone at the party, and of course, eating lots of cake!

PUFFCHEEK'S PALACE

WRITTEN BY GEOFF COWAN

If you walk carefully and quietly through a woodland dell, don't be startled to hear faint voices and glimpse some colourfully dressed little people. For there may be elves and pixies about, just like there were in the woods behind the garden of Kate's cottage home. Only, her brother Sam didn't believe her. Then something very strange happened that made him begin to wonder…

"Pull!" cried Topknot, sitting grandly on a small carriage he had found while going early-morning exploring.

He had fetched the other elves, and they were using a rope of woven grass to tow his discovery away. However, nothing much happened in those woods without the sharp-eyed pixies noticing. When they saw the carriage, they wanted to join in the fun.

"Push!" shouted Puffcheek to his fellow pixies.

So the elves pulled the carriage while the pixies pushed, until it lurched and Topknot almost fell off.

"Pulling's safer than pushing me along!" he called, grumpily.

"But pushing's easier, especially if you go downhill!" protested Puffcheek. "Watch! We'll show you!"

Before Topknot could stop them, Puffcheek and the other pixies gave such a mighty shove that the carriage suddenly sped forward. It moved so fast that the startled elves hardly had time to jump out of the way.

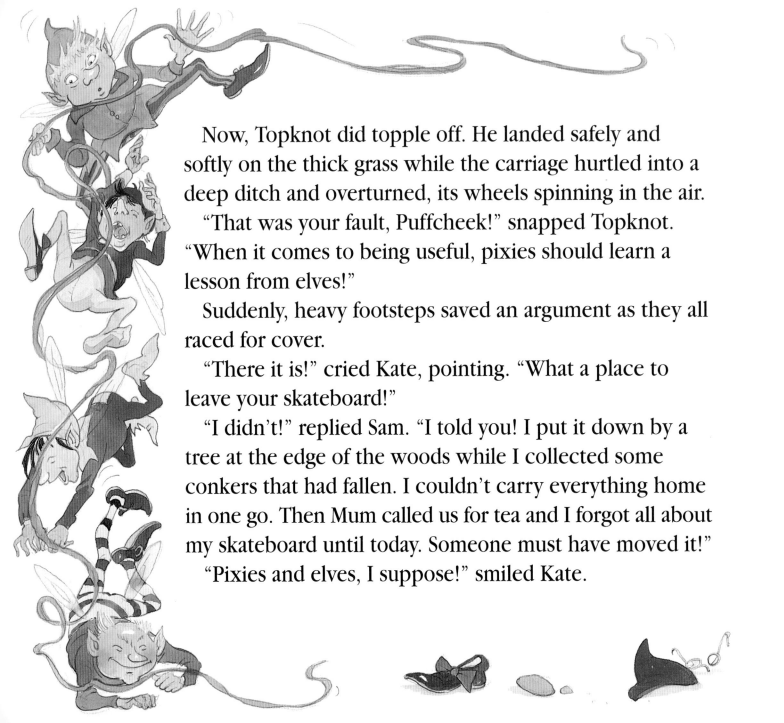

Now, Topknot did topple off. He landed safely and softly on the thick grass while the carriage hurtled into a deep ditch and overturned, its wheels spinning in the air.

"That was your fault, Puffcheek!" snapped Topknot. "When it comes to being useful, pixies should learn a lesson from elves!"

Suddenly, heavy footsteps saved an argument as they all raced for cover.

"There it is!" cried Kate, pointing. "What a place to leave your skateboard!"

"I didn't!" replied Sam. "I told you! I put it down by a tree at the edge of the woods while I collected some conkers that had fallen. I couldn't carry everything home in one go. Then Mum called us for tea and I forgot all about my skateboard until today. Someone must have moved it!"

"Pixies and elves, I suppose!" smiled Kate.

Sam laughed and scrambled into the ditch. He picked up his skateboard, then headed for home. Kate was about to follow when she spotted the elves' grass rope that had broken free from the skateboard. Kate looked at it thoughtfully and put it in her pocket.

"So that's where the carriage came from," said Topknot, afterwards.

"You mean skateboard," corrected Puffcheek. "The Big People use all kinds of odd things and give them some very funny names!"

"Well, whatever they call it, I want it back!" cried Topknot. "Finders keepers. That's only fair!"

Even the pixies agreed, so Puffcheek had no choice but to try and recover the skateboard.

Which brought him to Kate's cottage garden. Sam had already gone to meet a friend, taking the skateboard with him. Meanwhile, Kate sat at the far end of the garden to examine the little grass rope. Puffcheek crept closer, searching for the skateboard. Suddenly, Kate sneezed and blew the pixie off a log he had clambered on to.

"Hey! Look out, clumsy!" he yelled and Kate was just close enough to hear.

"Oh, there really are pixies," she cried. "Did you make this rope!"

"No, it was the elves!" replied Puffcheek, picking himself up.

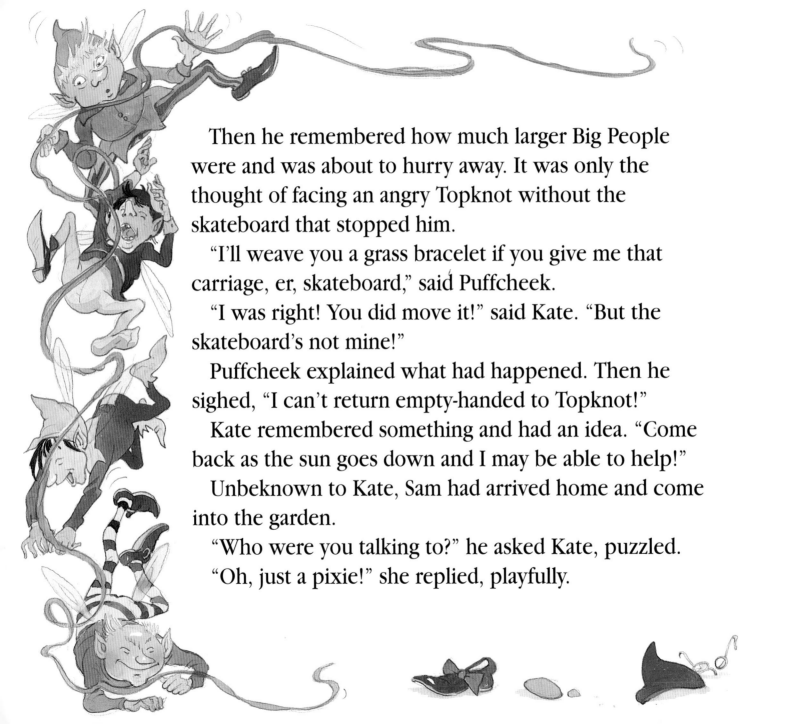

Then he remembered how much larger Big People were and was about to hurry away. It was only the thought of facing an angry Topknot without the skateboard that stopped him.

"I'll weave you a grass bracelet if you give me that carriage, er, skateboard," said Puffcheek.

"I was right! You did move it!" said Kate. "But the skateboard's not mine!"

Puffcheek explained what had happened. Then he sighed, "I can't return empty-handed to Topknot!"

Kate remembered something and had an idea. "Come back as the sun goes down and I may be able to help!"

Unbeknown to Kate, Sam had arrived home and come into the garden.

"Who were you talking to?" he asked Kate, puzzled.

"Oh, just a pixie!" she replied, playfully.

"You know you tidied up your cupboard yesterday. Didn't you say you wanted to get rid of your toy castle?" Kate asked.
Sam nodded. "I'm too big for it now!"

"I know someone who's just the right size!" said Kate. "Can I have it?"
"If you like," said Sam.

When Sam went inside, Kate fetched the little castle, complete with its turrets, drawbridge and battlements. She took it to the edge of the wood. At dusk, Puffcheek found the castle with a note from Kate telling him it was for Topknot.

"I'm sorry I was cross with you, Puffcheek!" said Topknot as, this time, the elves and pixies happily pushed and pulled the toy castle deeper into the woods. "A castle's better than a carriage any day!"

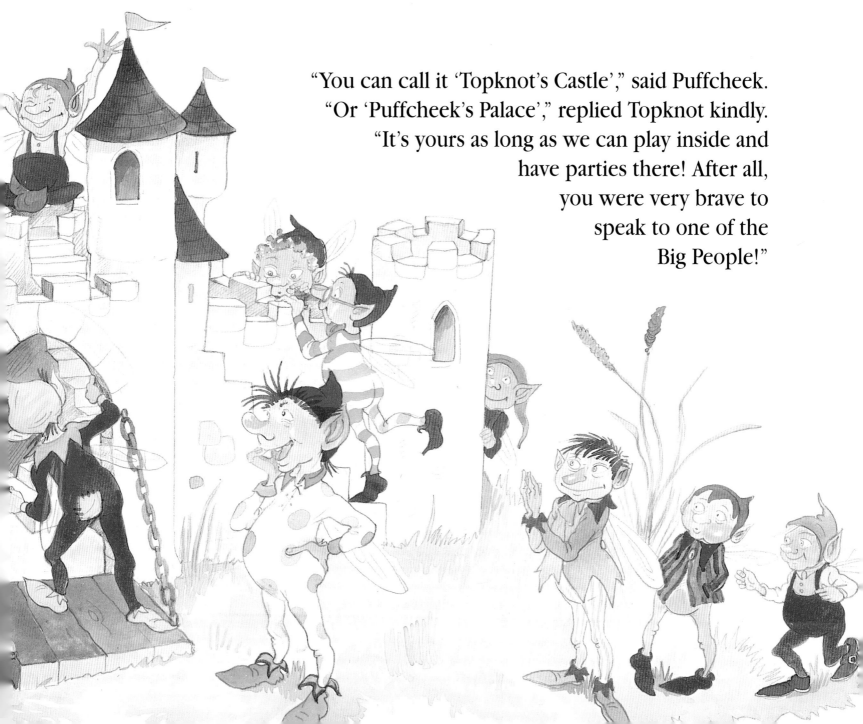

"You can call it 'Topknot's Castle'," said Puffcheek.
"Or 'Puffcheek's Palace'," replied Topknot kindly.
"It's yours as long as we can play inside and
have parties there! After all,
you were very brave to
speak to one of the
Big People!"

Puffcheek smiled proudly as the elves and pixies congratulated him.

Next morning, before school, Sam followed his sister into the garden.

"I saw you carrying my castle down to the bottom of the garden last night," he said. "You wanted to play with it yourself all along, didn't you?"

"No, I left it here," replied Kate, pointing. "But it's gone!"

"Just like my skateboard," said Sam, thoughtfully. "Shall we search for it?"

"No," replied Kate, who was very pleased to have helped Puffcheek and the others.

"Don't tell me you think the elves and pixies took my old toy castle too!" grinned Sam.

Kate nodded. "Who else?" she smiled. "Only, this time, I think we'll let them keep it!"

DRAGON HIS HEELS

WRITTEN BY DAN ABNETT

There once was a land, not too far from where you live, which was ruled by an old king. The old king was very happy with his kingdom. It had mountains, and lakes, and forests, and a castle or two, and just the right amount of strange creatures to make it a proper fairytale kingdom. This suited the old king right down to the ground, as he was a proper fairytale king, and he took a pride in his work.

Once a month, he took down his Great Big Account

Book and ticked off the bits and pieces of his kingdom. A wishing well (tick!), a unicorn (tick!), a fountain of youth (tick!), five fairies (tick!), a wicked witch (part time, Tuesdays and Thursdays only … tick!), four fierce lions (tick! tick! tick! tick!), a pack of wolves (tick!), a family of hill giants (tick!), two dragons (tick! and tick!), and a young prince/heir to the throne/son type thing (…er…tick!).

It was a busy time for the old king. Proper fairytale kingdoms don't just run themselves, you know. There was always something to fix. If it wasn't the wicked witch asking for an extra morning off, it was the wishing well wishing it was something else, like a public telephone box for instance. That had taken some sorting out, I can tell you. It's all very well getting an operator who says, "your wish is my command," but you just try dialling up a casket of gold, a magic sword and a beautiful princess after six o'clock.

Anyway, one particular month, the old king sat with the Great Big Account Book across his knobbly old fairytale knees and noticed another thing that needed fixing.

"Oh, blow and tish!" said the old king. "Tish" is a very rude word in proper fairytale kingdoms, and only old kings are allowed to say it.

Already that morning he'd sorted out the go-slow at Tallboy and Sons Ltd, and helped elect a new leader for the wolf pack (the last one had left to go on a werewolfing course). But when he got to "two dragons" (tick!), he noticed that the account book now read, "three dragons."

He didn't, of course, tick that. Three dragons was far too many for a small fairytale kingdom, even if it was a proper one. Three dragons was excessive. Three dragons was… a dragon too many. It said so in his *How to Rule a Proper Fairytale Kingdom* manual.

"We," said the old king, using the royal "we" (something else that only old kings are allowed to do), "will have to do something about this quick smart!"

The old king sent for his son. He was sure he had one of those young prince/heir to the throne/son type of things. He'd ticked one off himself only the month before. Between you and me, the old king was a little concerned about the young prince. There were certain things a young prince had to do if he wanted to stay in the job, and this young prince hadn't shown signs of doing any of them. "Well, that's about to change," said the old king to himself.

The young prince came when called, and smiled at the old king in a friendly way.

"I want you to seek out a dragon and kill it," said the old king.

"Pardon, Dad?" the young prince said.

"I want you to seek out a dragon and kill it," repeated the old king. "We've got far too many, and that's what young princes do. And don't call me 'Dad.' It's undignified. Call me your Highness."

"Okay," said the young prince, a little confused. "About this dragon … why have I got to kill it?"

"We've got too many of them. And it says here in my manual that young princes are supposed to seek out and dispose of any excess dragons. It's part of their job."

So off went the young prince. He wasn't too happy about it. He'd never killed anything in his young and princely life, and he wasn't really sure he wanted to.

But he put on his silver armour, collected his lance and his white charger, and off he went. He looked terrific, just like a young prince should do. Even the wicked witch approved (it was, mind you, her day off).

After a long journey, the young prince arrived

at the place on his map marked 'Here Be Dragons.' He got down from his white charger and walked towards a cave.

"Hello? Dragons? Are you home?" he called into the cave.

"Hold on," said a voice. "I'll be right out."

After a moment, a dragon came out of the cave. It wasn't a very big dragon at all, and the young prince was quite disappointed (and rather pleased at the same time). The dragon was no taller than the prince, but it was a real dragon. It had a mouthful of long fangs, a tail that ended in a little arrowhead spike, a coat of the most splendid green scales, and a pair of tiny wings. When it spoke, little flames crackled along its forked tongue.

"And you are?" asked the small dragon.

"The young prince," said the young prince.

"Pleased to meet you. I'm the small dragon," said the small dragon. They shook hands, and the small dragon offered the young prince a glass of lemonade, which was thoughtful of him, as the young prince had ridden a fair distance and was thirsty. They sat and sipped their lemonade. The young prince was particularly impressed by the way the small dragon stuck out his littlest claw as he held the glass. A sign of polite breeding, his father would have said.

"So what can I do for you, Young Prince?" asked the small dragon. "I'm afraid my mum and dad, the big dragons, are out at the moment. Princesses to menace, villages to burn with their flaming breath … you know how it is."

"Well, you see, the thing is …" began the young prince. "Actually, I've got to find a dragon and kill it. Dad says I must."

"Oh!" said the small dragon.

"Sorry," said the young prince.

"Must you?" said the small dragon.

"'Fraid so," said the young prince.

"I wouldn't want you to disobey your dad, of course, but is there any way we could skip the actual 'killing a dragon' bit?" asked the small dragon.

"I don't know," said the young prince, thoughtfully. "It depends. Can you play hide and seek?"

When the young prince got home, the old king had the Great Big Account Book open on his famously knobbly knees.

"Dragons?" he asked, sternly.

"Two," said the young prince.

"Tick! Well done! Young prince/heir to the throne/son type of things who do what they're asked to do?" asked the old king.

"One. Right here," said the young prince.

"Tick!" said the old king happily, ticking.

"You'd better add a new bit to your accounts, though, your Highness," said the young prince after a pause.

"And what would that be?" asked the old king, starting a new page and reaching for his ruler.

"Friends of the young prince/heir to the throne/son type of thing," said the young prince.

"How many?" asked the old king.

"One," said the prince, smiling.

"Made a friend, did you?" asked the old king, closing the Great Big Account Book and looking up with a smile.

"Yes," said the young prince. "One who's much better at hiding than I am at seeking."

And from that day on, there have been the right number of ticks in the old king's book.

THE LOST GIANT

WRITTEN BY AMBER HUNT

The air wobbled a bit, shimmered, swirled and with a 'whoomph' a rather bewildered, twelve-foot giant appeared. He was only a very young giant, and looked rather like any other young boy — except he was slightly larger, of course!

"Oh dear," said the giant, stepping on a bush and flattening it. Turning round he bumped into a tree, which bent over at an alarming angle.

"Hello," said a tiny voice.

"What was that?!" said the giant, startled. He whirled round looking for the voice and knocked the tree right over. "Where am I?"

"Stand still," yelled the small voice. "You're in our farmyard. I suspect you are all my fault!"

"Pardon?" said the giant. "Did you say I'm all your fault?"

"Yes," yelled the small voice. "Only could you whisper because you are deafening me."

"Of course," apologised the giant and stepping back he trod in the pond and got his socks wet.

"Stand still please, before you demolish the whole farmyard," pleaded the voice.

"Where are you?" asked the giant.

"I'm down here, by the well. Perhaps if you bend down, carefully, you might be able to see me."

And so, carefully, the giant bent down and peered at the well. Standing next to it was a little boy with blond hair and very dirty knees.

"Oh," said the giant. "You're a little boy … aren't you afraid of me? All the little boys in my story books are afraid of giants." "No, I'm not afraid," said the little boy.

The giant got down on his hands and knees to get a closer look. "Gosh, your knees are dirty," he said. "Have you been playing?"

The little boy looked at his knees. "Um, yes, I suppose they are a bit dirty. I lost my magic marble and was crawling around looking for it. This is a farmyard you know, so it gets a bit muddy."

"Oh," breathed the giant. "Have you got a magic marble? I've got one too. Here look," and he fished a marble as big as a doughnut out of his pocket.

"Wow," said the little boy. "That's wonderful. I wish I could find mine." Then a thought crossed his mind. "How old are you?" he asked the giant.

"Seventy," replied the giant.

"Oh," said the little boy, clearly disappointed.

"But I think ten giant years are the same as one of your years, so I suppose I'm about seven in your world."

"I'm seven too!" said the little boy, "That's, terrific! You know what, I think my marble magicked you here. I was wishing for someone to play with when the air went wobbly. I was so scared I dropped my marble, which was why I was crawling around in the mud looking for it — and then you appeared. What's your name?" he asked. "Mine's Oliver."

"I'm Bertie," said the giant. "I was wishing for a friend on my marble too," and they looked at each other in awe.

"Wow," they breathed together. "Weird!"

Just then a voice called from inside the farmhouse," Oliver, Oliver!"

"Oh, no," said Oliver, "that's my mum. You'd better hide quickly." Oliver looked at his large friend. Where on earth do you hide a twelve-foot giant?

"I've got it," he said, "in the barn. Follow me — very carefully."

Oliver ran across the yard, with Bertie following — carefully. They went down past the stables, across the cornfield and into the meadow where the hay barn was.

"Oliver, Oliver, where are you? It's lunchtime." His mum's voice floated across the meadow.

"Quick, help me with this door," panted Oliver. Bertie heaved open the hay barn door and dived inside.

"Good, there's plenty of space. Hide over there in that corner. Well, as best you can, anyway. I have to go and have my lunch," Oliver explained to Bertie, "then I'll come back. Are you hungry?" he added.

Bertie nodded silently, afraid that if he spoke Oliver's mother might hear him. He couldn't stop his tummy rumbling though. It sounded just like thunder.

"I'll try and get you something to eat," Oliver promised and off he went, back to the house for lunch. He gobbled his lunch up as quickly as he could. He could hardly wait to get back to the barn and see his new friend. As soon as he finished eating he rushed back to Bertie.

He had brought Bertie a jam sandwich, which he'd hidden in his pocket. Bertie ate it in one bite. He was too polite to tell Oliver that giants make their sandwiches as big as double beds.

"Now," said Oliver, "we have to find my marble and a way to get you back home. You're too big to stay here and Dad said he had some work to do later in the barn — so we'd better hurry."

Bertie and Oliver crept out of the barn and back to the well. They both got down on their hands and knees and started searching for the marble. They searched and searched, but found nothing.

Eventually Bertie said, "I'm thirsty. Is there any water in your well?" He peered over the edge.

"No," said Oliver, "it's been filled in."

"Wait a minute," yelled the giant, causing the ground to shake and the trees to sway dangerously, "I think I've found it! There's something shining in the earth, about three feet down," and he reached his long arm into the well, fished around a bit and brought out — the marble!

"Hooray! You've found it!" cried Oliver.

"Wow," gasped Bertie. "It's beautiful."

"Right, back to the barn," said Oliver excitedly. "It's time for some magic!"

Back in the barn Oliver and Bertie sat and rubbed their marbles and tried all the magic words they could think of, but the air didn't move, no 'whoomph' sound happened and Bertie stayed firmly in the barn with Oliver.

"Bertie," said Oliver, "would you like to swap marbles — like best friends do? We might even find a way to visit each other." Bertie nodded, smiling enthusiastically, "I'd like you to visit me in the land of the giants," he said.

In the distance Oliver could hear a tractor. "Oh no," he said. "I think my Dad might be coming. We have to think of something, quickly!"

They rubbed the marbles harder and started to invent magic words and all the time the tractor was getting nearer. How would Oliver explain keeping a twelve-foot giant in the barn?

Then Bertie had an idea. "The air went 'whoomph' when I arrived, didn't it? So perhaps if we made the noise backwards it might magic me home."

Oliver and Bertie looked at each other.

"Bye," said Oliver, rubbing his eyes. "See you again?"

"Bye," said Bertie, sniffing. "I'll come back soon."

Oliver and Bertie rubbed their marbles hard, and together they said "Phmoohw." The air wobbled and shimmered a bit and in a flash Bertie was gone.

Outside the tractor noise stopped and a few seconds later Oliver's Dad walked into the barn. "Hello," he said. "What are you doing here? That's a pretty amazing marble," he added, nodding at Oliver's hand.

"Yes it is, isn't it?" Oliver held up the marble, which was as big as a doughnut, for his dad to see. "It's a giant-size one," he said, and smiled secretly to himself.

A NASTY CASE OF GOBLINS

WRITTEN BY DAN ABNETT

Lord Dubloon of Steep Castle took a step back in amazement. "I've g...got wh..what?" he stammered.

The dwarf from the Council straightened the front of his overalls and tucked his stubby pencil behind his stubby ear. "You've got the worst case of goblins I've ever seen in all my long years."

Lord Dubloon's legs suddenly decided he needed to sit down, and he staggered backwards onto his huge chair. "Goblins?" he asked. "In my castle?"

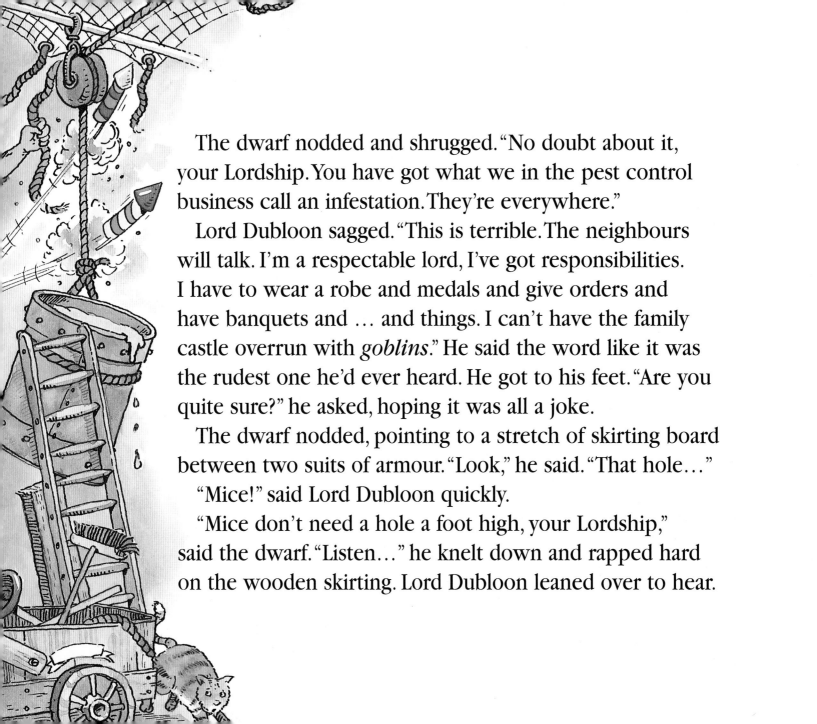

The dwarf nodded and shrugged. "No doubt about it, your Lordship. You have got what we in the pest control business call an infestation. They're everywhere."

Lord Dubloon sagged. "This is terrible. The neighbours will talk. I'm a respectable lord, I've got responsibilities. I have to wear a robe and medals and give orders and have banquets and … and things. I can't have the family castle overrun with *goblins*." He said the word like it was the rudest one he'd ever heard. He got to his feet. "Are you quite sure?" he asked, hoping it was all a joke.

The dwarf nodded, pointing to a stretch of skirting board between two suits of armour. "Look," he said. "That hole…"

"Mice!" said Lord Dubloon quickly.

"Mice don't need a hole a foot high, your Lordship," said the dwarf. "Listen…" he knelt down and rapped hard on the wooden skirting. Lord Dubloon leaned over to hear.

The unmistakable sound of cackling laughter floated up out of the hole. Goblins, sniggering. The dwarf looked up at Lord Dubloon.

"Goblins," he stated, somewhat shortly.

Lord Dubloon sighed and thought for a while. "Can you do anything about them?" he asked.

The dwarf frowned and whistled through his teeth. "No," he said, at last. "But," he added, "I know a dwarf who can."

A second dwarf arrived at Steep Castle the next morning, pushing a handcart with a sign painted on the side. The sign read:

"Short Brothers, Pest Control. Biggest in the business. Gorgons, Goblins and Cockroaches a speciality." Lord Dubloon hurried outside. "Lord Dubloon! A pleasure!" said Mr Short smartly. "They tell me it's goblins you've got."

Lord Dubloon nodded.

"Right ho!" said the dwarf. He put on a pair of big leather gloves, a pair of rubber waders, a welding mask and goggles, and a hardhat with a miner's lamp attached to it.

"Mmmgg mghhmmp ggmmgp hhgg," he said.

"Pardon?" asked Lord Dubloon.

Mr Short raised the visor of his welding mask. "Show me the way!" he repeated. "And could you give me a hand with my equipment?"

Weighed down with ropes and ladders and sink plungers and butterfly nets, Lord Dubloon led Mr Short into the Grand Hall.

The dwarf dropped onto his hands and knees and crawled over to the hole in the skirting board. He tapped at the wood. They heard goblin laughter.

"Down to business," said Mr Short.

Later that morning, Lord Dubloon returned to the Grand Hall to see how things were going. Mr Short had certainly been busy. All the furniture had been pushed back and covered with dust sheets, and scaffolding had been erected along the wall over the hole in the skirting board. Pulleys and ropes held a huge net across the roof, and other ropes ran down to the floor, where they were trapped under a large cast iron tub. The tub itself was perched on the end of a plank of wood that was balanced on a barrel like a see-saw. High above, Lord Dubloon's chair dangled from the scaffolding on a rope. In another corner of the room was a rack of fireworks. Mr Short sat under the scaffolding, slowly fitting together a long, flexible pole.

Lord Dubloon edged across to the tub perched on the see-saw and looked in. It was full of custard.

"Careful there, your Lordship. Custard. Very precarious. This whole apparatus is on a hair trigger."

"What is all this?" asked Lord Dubloon.

"Short's Patent Goblin Trap," replied Mr Short, proudly. "Allow me to explain. They love custard, do goblins, can't get enough of it. They come out of their hole to get to the custard. I light the fireworks. Boom! Bang! Whizz! Very pretty. Goblins love fireworks too. So they're all stood round the custard tub, and they're looking up admiring the fireworks. But … one of the fireworks is aimed at the rope holding the throne. It cuts through it. The throne drops onto the see-saw, the tub flies into the air, covering the goblins in sticky custard. They can't move, and the net floats down and traps them. Bingo!"

Lord Dubloon nodded, uncertainly. "So why do they come out of the hole in the first place?" he asked.

Mr Short held up the long, flexible pole. On the end was a sign that said: "HEY! GOBLINS! CUSTARD! THIS WAY!"

"This will fetch them out," said Mr Short. "Now, would you be so kind as to poke this pole down the hole?"

Lord Dubloon did so, as Mr Short stood by the fireworks with a lighted match. Lord Dubloon suddenly felt the pole being tugged out of his hands. It disappeared into the hole. Hearing excited goblin voices, he backed away. A moment later, a dozen little, green, pointy-eared, fanged, wicked, giggling goblins came rushing out of the skirting board, and headed straight for the custard.

"Bingo!" cried Mr Short, and lit the fireworks. They went off with a bang. It all happened very quickly. The goblins went "Oooohhh!" as they looked up at the fireworks shooting madly around the hall. Then they picked up the tub and ran for the hole in the skirting board. One firework released the chair, which crashed down and shattered, pinging the see-saw through a window with a loud crash.

The net was already falling. Mr Short, who was being chased by a firework, caught his foot in a stray rope and disappeared up to the ceiling, where he dangled upside down. Lord Dubloon looked at the devastation that had been his Grand Hall. He wanted to sit down, but his chair had been smashed into firewood.

Just then, the flexible pole poked back out of the goblin hole with a very badly written note on the end of it. It read: "tHAnkS FoRe ThE cUSTaRd. yOr. KloWn wAs vERy FUnnY. mAkE hIm dO It AgAin."

Fuming, Lord Dubloon looked up at Mr Short. "Bingo?"

"Just a temporary setback, your Lordship," began Mr Short. "Er… do you think you could help me down from here?"

Lord Dubloon winced as the echoes of goblin laughter floated out from the skirting board. "I'll make 'short' work of you when I do!"

GNOME SWEET GNOME

WRITTEN BY DAN ABNETT

Just west of the snow-capped Candlemass Mountains, at the point where the Great West Road crosses the Green River, you'll find a little pottery business run by a family of gnomes called the Slightlys. These gnomes are kind, generous little people, no taller than a chair leg. They never shout or say rude words or pull hair, they never leave things in a mess and they never have a bad word to say about anyone.

Gnomes are great craftsmen, and the Slightlys are no exception. They have owned the little pottery for years

making the finest teapots, bowls, dishes and jugs you'll ever see. Travellers often stop and buy something from the Slightlys' shop. Each item of Gnomeware comes packed in straw in a little wooden box with a label that reads "Slightly Gnome-made".

Mr Slightly is the master potter, and spends all day in the workshop, making the Gnomeware on his potter's wheel. His sister, Everso Slightly, is in charge of the kiln, where she bakes the soft pottery until it's hard. Mrs Slightly and her daughter, Very, paint lovely patterns on the Gnomeware, and glaze them shiny and bright, and Grandma and Grandpa Slightly run the shop.

Then of course, there's young Od. He's Mr Slightly's son, and a fine young figure of a gnome.

It had always been assumed that Od Slightly would follow in the family footsteps and one day become the master potter himself. Every day he studied as an apprentice in the workshop. Trouble was, try as he might, Od wasn't very keen on pot-making. He just didn't have his father's patience, or his steady hand. Od's dishes always looked a little wobbly. The handles fell off his jugs, the lids never fitted his bowls, and he was forever getting confused and putting two spouts on his teapots. More than once, he'd lost control of the potter's wheel completely, and sent wet, floppy clay splatting all over the nice clean workshop.

Whenever things went wrong, Od's father would stand with his hands on his hips, shaking his head sadly. Mrs Slightly would say, "There, there, Od," and go and fetch the dustpan and mop. Very Slightly, who could paint patterns on the Gnomeware every bit as well as her mum, would snigger at her brother in a very superior way.

All day long, Od dreamed fantastic dreams of high adventure and peril. He was Od the Pirate Gnome, Od the Jungle Explorer, Od the Racing car Driver, Od the Test Pilot… he had a stack of old *Ideal Gnome* magazines, which were full of articles about high fliers in the gnome world. Film star gnomes and secret agent gnomes and million pound-transfer footballer gnomes called Gnozza. "One day…" he'd say to himself, as he sponged clay-blobs off the workshop wall, "…one day I'll pack my things, leave this miserable, boring, clay-filled life and go off to seek my fortune. I'll become Very Famous Gnome Celebrity Od Slightly and send exciting postcards home to mum and dad. Just let Very snigger at me then." As an afterthought, he added to himself, "I'll probably have to change my name, though, if I'm going to be a Very Famous Gnome Celebrity. Something like Brad Slightly or Rock Slightly would sound more cool."

One particular morning, Od's latest edition of *Ideal Gnome* magazine arrived in the post. In the classified section was an advert that quite took Od's breath away.

"Good-looking young gnomes required for ornamental duties. Apply to the Royal Palace of King Barnabus II."

When Mr Slightly got up for work, he couldn't find Od anywhere. He checked the house and the workshop, but Od was nowhere to be found. Then Aunt Everso found a note pinned to the kiln. "Gone to seek fortune. Have taken clean underwear. Will write soon." It was signed, "Od."

"Oh dear me…" murmured Mrs Slightly.

It took Od three days to reach the palace of King Barnabus II. He was tired and weary by the time he arrived at the gates. If it hadn't been for the lift he'd got for the last ten miles on the back of an ox cart, he was sure he'd never have made it.

The palace was huge, even by gnome standards. Little Od looked around in awe. Big people marched about the place being important. Trumpets blasted out fanfares that made him jump out of his shoes. He had to scurry out of the way of enormous, stomping soldiers, and horses on parade. Even the dwarf footmen looked down on him.

Eventually he found his way to the Lord Chamberlain's office and knocked nervously at the door. "Come in," boomed a deep voice from inside. The Chamberlain peered down at him over the top of his glasses with a scornful sneer, and dabbed his pen in the inkpot. "Name?"

"Erm… Shane Slightly," said Od, in a rather shaky voice. He was trembling so hard that his knees knocked together.

"Slightly… hmmm," said the Chamberlain, writing it down in a big book. "And you're here for the gnome job?"

"The ornamental one, that's right, sir," said Od with

a friendly grin. The chamberlain didn't smile back. Od didn't really know what the job was about, but he reckoned that if it was ornamental, it probably meant he was going to be a gnome model. Maybe he'd be paid millions and appear on the cover of glamorous fashion magazines.

"Follow me," said the Chamberlain, and led him through the huge palace gardens and down to the lake. He handed Od a small fishing rod.

"Sit there," he said, pointing to a rock on the lake edge, "and pretend to fish."

"Is that all?" asked Od.

"You'll work from sunrise until sunset, unless there's an evening garden party, in which case you work overtime. On no account are you to move, wander about or do anything except look ornamental." The Chamberlain stomped off and left Od to it. Od sat down on the rock, feeling rather uneasy.

Two hours later, he still felt uneasy, but now he felt hot and uncomfortable too. He was bored. His neck was stiff, and there was an annoying fly buzzing around his ear. The Chamberlain came back to check on him.

"Very good, but try smiling too," he said.

"What do I do when I've finished this?" asked Od.

"What do you mean, 'finish'," replied the Chamberlain, looking taken aback. "This is what you're paid to do. You're an ornamental garden gnome."

Od was halfway home, trudging along the Great West Road, when he met Grandpa Slightly coming the other way.

"Thought I might find you out here, young Od," said Grandpa. They fell into step, heading back towards the Candlemass Mountains, where the sun was just setting. "You know, more than anything else, I want to make a big teapot," said Od. "I've really got the urge."

"That's the spirit," said Grandpa.
Od thought a while, then said, "I've decided, Grandpa.
Wherever you go, there's really no place like gnome."

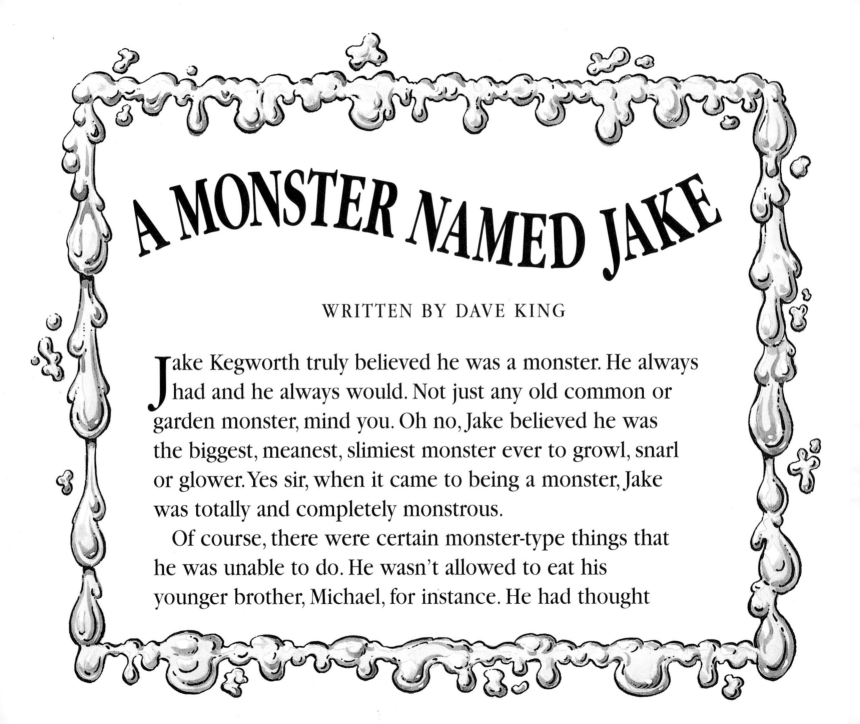

A MONSTER NAMED JAKE

WRITTEN BY DAVE KING

Jake Kegworth truly believed he was a monster. He always had and he always would. Not just any old common or garden monster, mind you. Oh no, Jake believed he was the biggest, meanest, slimiest monster ever to growl, snarl or glower. Yes sir, when it came to being a monster, Jake was totally and completely monstrous.

Of course, there were certain monster-type things that he was unable to do. He wasn't allowed to eat his younger brother, Michael, for instance. He had thought

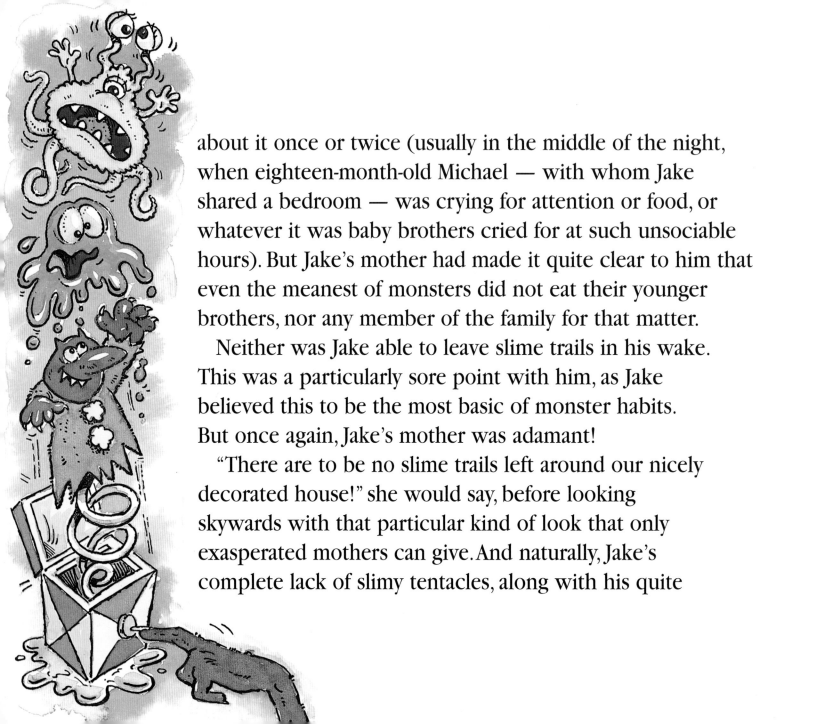

about it once or twice (usually in the middle of the night, when eighteen-month-old Michael — with whom Jake shared a bedroom — was crying for attention or food, or whatever it was baby brothers cried for at such unsociable hours). But Jake's mother had made it quite clear to him that even the meanest of monsters did not eat their younger brothers, nor any member of the family for that matter.

Neither was Jake able to leave slime trails in his wake. This was a particularly sore point with him, as Jake believed this to be the most basic of monster habits. But once again, Jake's mother was adamant!

"There are to be no slime trails left around our nicely decorated house!" she would say, before looking skywards with that particular kind of look that only exasperated mothers can give. And naturally, Jake's complete lack of slimy tentacles, along with his quite normal amount of eyes, arms, legs and so on, did put something of a damper on his efforts to scare the living daylights out of Mrs Ricklesworth, his elderly next door neighbour. (Jake was, of course, a young monster, so his view of Mrs Ricklesworth's age was not quite accurate. In everybody else's eyes — including her own — she was in her late forties.) No matter how often he waved his arms about, or writhed and wriggled his fingers in what Jake felt was a distinctly creepy manner, Mrs Ricklesworth remained quite unnervingly cool.

"Ah!" Jake thought, in his darkest moments. "But if I had even one purple tentacle, things would be very different. Oh yes!"

Despite all this, Jake still believed himself to be much better at being a monster than anybody else he knew — although he would occasionally and grudgingly admit to

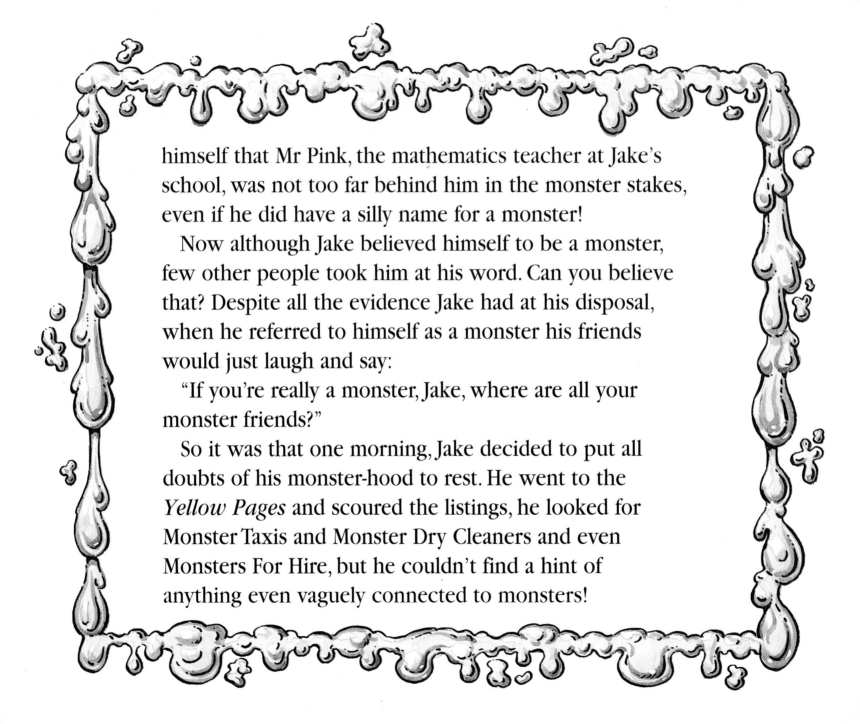

himself that Mr Pink, the mathematics teacher at Jake's school, was not too far behind him in the monster stakes, even if he did have a silly name for a monster!

Now although Jake believed himself to be a monster, few other people took him at his word. Can you believe that? Despite all the evidence Jake had at his disposal, when he referred to himself as a monster his friends would just laugh and say:

"If you're really a monster, Jake, where are all your monster friends?"

So it was that one morning, Jake decided to put all doubts of his monster-hood to rest. He went to the *Yellow Pages* and scoured the listings, he looked for Monster Taxis and Monster Dry Cleaners and even Monsters For Hire, but he couldn't find a hint of anything even vaguely connected to monsters!

His friends, watching from outside the window, were most curious to know why Jake was looking so intently through the phone book.

"Perhaps he's going mad?" one of them suggested.

They were even more bewildered when Jake let out a yelp of delight and began jumping around the room in a most peculiar manner. They watched as he dashed to the telephone and made a call. When Jake had finished, one of his friends tapped on the window. Jake rushed over, threw the window open and declared,

"You are all invited to tea on Saturday, when I shall prove to you once and for all that I am a monster!"

Naturally enough, word spread around the town that something was going to be happening on Saturday and everyone became excited at the thought of Jake making a very large fool of himself.

"Perhaps this will finally free the poor boy from the crazy idea that he is a monster! It would make my life a lot more peaceful, I can tell you!" Mrs Ricklesworth said to her good friend,

Mrs Parker (about whom we shall perhaps talk some other time, when you will learn of the fate that befell her husband during an attempt to cross the English Channel on a raft made of sponge-cake).

Saturday came (as Saturdays do) and brought with it a large crowd of interested onlookers gathering around the Kegworth household. The crowd became more and more excited as the afternoon wore on, calling for proof of Jake's monster status. In fact, they became so loud that Jake's poor mother developed the most frightful headache!

Jake's friends arrived for tea at five minutes before four o'clock, each of them looking a little nervous, if truth be told (and of course, it is). And at four o'clock precisely, everyone, including Mrs Ricklesworth, Jake's family and friends and all of the interested onlookers, fell into a hushed silence. What was about to happen? What was Jake about to do?

By five minutes after four, the crowd was getting restless, and murmurs of "I told you so," could be heard. Nothing had happened, of course! How silly of them to think that something would. Poor Jake was beginning to look a little green (which is something that all good monsters know how to do, by the way).

Just then, a large, brightly painted coach drew up outside the house. And what do you think happened? Well, I'll tell you… the coach doors opened and out walked the most revolting bunch of monsters you've never wanted to see (or perhaps you have, in which case you may well be a monster, too!)

They were slimy, nasty, icky and yucky looking, with all kinds of tentacles, claws, eyes on stalks, lumps and bumps. It's fairly safe to say, that they were an unbelievably ugly bunch, even by monster standards, and they're pretty low!

They made their way up the garden path and Jake opened the front door.

"Hello, my friends!" he said. "How nice to meet you all at last! Do come in and have some tea!"

"Hello, Jake!" said the biggest monster, through at least sixteen mouths. "I hope you've got some chocolate biscuits, because as you probably know, monsters simply adore chocolate biscuits!"

Sure enough, Jake had chocolate biscuits, along with all kinds of other nice things to eat. They all sat down to tea, and neither Jake's family, his friends nor the rest of the town, ever doubted again that Jake was a true monster! After all, who else but a monster would invite other monsters to tea?

Now you might be wondering how Jake eventually contacted the other monsters? It was really very simple, he looked in the phone book under "Clubs and Associations" and found the number for the "Monster Society and Social Club". If you'd like, you can give them a call and invite some monsters round for tea, but you'd probably best check with your mother first, because as Jake's mother found, monsters really do leave slime trails everywhere they go!

FAIRY DUST DILEMMA!

WRITTEN BY DAVE KING

Florence was not a happy fairy. She had spent the whole day turning her house upside down. Not literally, of course, as that would cause more problems than it solved. No, Florence had been searching through cupboards and drawers, looking in boxes and digging into nooks and crannies. All in pursuit of one particular and very special thing… fairy dust!

Now Florence had not been a fairy for very long. In fact she had only graduated from the School for Gifted Fairies,

Elves and Pixies a matter of weeks ago, which was all the more reason why her present predicament was so embarrassing.

If she was an old fairy, she would perhaps have some excuse for her forgetfulness. But to have forgotten where or how to make fairy dust so soon after graduating… well, she would probably never live it down if anyone ever found out.

The day had begun well enough. Florence had been flitting around the flower beds of one of the local parks, making sure that all the flowers were tended to (Florence, you see, was a fully qualified Flower Fairy).

Just as she was taking off from a particularly high daffodil — fairies aren't very tall, don't forget — she suddenly felt a very peculiar, tingling sensation. And with that, she fell to the ground, landing in a patch of muddy soil. As a rule, fairies don't like getting muddy and Florence was no exception. In fact, she positively hated it!

Florence sat grumpily in the mud, wondering what could possibly have made her fall. She got up, brushed herself down as best she could and leapt daintily into the air once more… only to land, splat, face first in the mud!

"Oh bother!" she said (although, with a mouthful of mud it sounded more like "Bob blobber!" which, if you ask me, is a very peculiar thing to say).

For some reason it seemed she was unable to fly, so Florence began to walk home. She looked a fine sight, covered from head to foot with mud. Florence wished she could clean the mud off and, as if in answer to her wishes, it began to rain. It came down gently at first, almost a fine mist, but by the time Florence reached home, it was pouring down in torrents.

Florence walked into her house and plopped down on the stairs, feeling very miserable.

"I'm feeling very miserable!" she stated, to no one in particular. Fairies have a nasty habit of stating the obvious.

Once she had dried herself off and changed her clothes, Florence moved into the kitchen and went over to the bookshelf.

"Now where did I put that book?" she said. "I was only looking at it yesterday, so it can't have gone too far!" The book in question was the *Big Book of Fairy Facts, Figures, Spells, Potions and Cookery Tips*, a very useful book which no self-respecting fairy would be seen dead without.

"I simply have to find it!" Florence snapped, as she stomped from one room to another. And then she remembered, she had been reading the book whilst taking a bath! She rushed upstairs to the bathroom and then remembered something else… she had dropped the book into the bath. It lay on the window ledge. Some of the pages had stuck together and the rest had gone quite crinkly, but she was still able to find the section she was looking for.

She read through the section on flight most intently. Eventually, she leapt up. "Ah ha!" she said. "Fairy dust, of course! How could I forget?"

Fairy dust was the magic substance which gave fairies the power of flight, amongst other things. "Now then," she said, "all I have to do is find the section on how to make fairy dust! I hope I've got the right ingredients."

She flipped through the book, only to discover that the chapter on fairy dust was well and truly stuck together, and no amount of prising, pulling, tugging or tearing was going to pull the pages apart. "Oh, puddlesticks!" Florence shouted, stamping her feet.

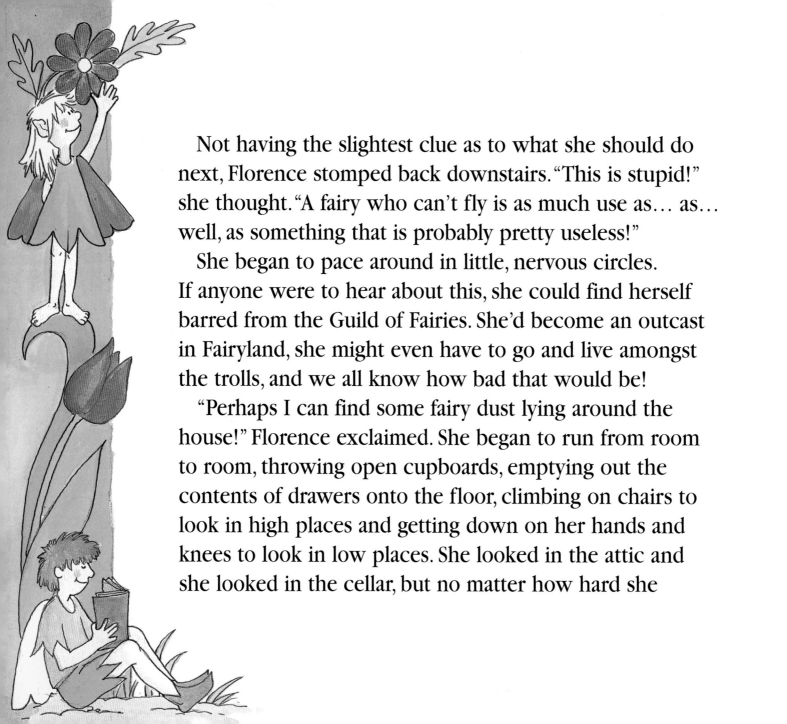

Not having the slightest clue as to what she should do next, Florence stomped back downstairs. "This is stupid!" she thought. "A fairy who can't fly is as much use as… as… well, as something that is probably pretty useless!"

She began to pace around in little, nervous circles. If anyone were to hear about this, she could find herself barred from the Guild of Fairies. She'd become an outcast in Fairyland, she might even have to go and live amongst the trolls, and we all know how bad that would be!

"Perhaps I can find some fairy dust lying around the house!" Florence exclaimed. She began to run from room to room, throwing open cupboards, emptying out the contents of drawers onto the floor, climbing on chairs to look in high places and getting down on her hands and knees to look in low places. She looked in the attic and she looked in the cellar, but no matter how hard she looked, she simply could not find what she was looking for. Of course, it might have helped if she could have remembered just what fairy dust looked like. It has to be said that Florence really was a rather forgetful fairy.

Florence burst into tears. "Waaaaaaaahhh!!" she cried. Just then, the doorbell went. Florence looked horrified. She didn't want anyone to see her like this, so she tidied herself up and answered the door.

It was her best friend, Phyllis. "Hello!" Phyllis said. "And how are…" was all she managed to say before Florence grabbed her and dragged her inside. "Phyllis, I'm so glad it's you!" Florence gasped. "You have to help me!"

Phyllis told Florence that she would be only too glad to help, if she would only tell her why she was so upset and why the house looked like a horde of trolls had been using it to play a game of five-a-side football.

"You silly banana!" Phyllis replied upon hearing Florence's predicament. "The answer's been under your nose all along!" And with that, she took her friend over to the bookshelf, and wiped her finger along it. "Fairy dust," she said, holding aloft a dust covered finger, "is simply the dust that gathers in the homes of all fairies!"

And so, if you should ever find yourself in a fairy's house, you'll know why the dusting never seems to get done!